AF254331

# ESCAPING THE STORM

## BOOK FOUR OF THE STORM SERIES

SHANE KROETSCH

Escaping the Storm

Copyright © Shane Kroetsch



First edition February 2026



This story is a work of fiction. Names, characters, places, and incidents are either the product of the author's imagination or are used fictitiously. Any resemblance to actual persons, living or undead, or actual events, is coincidental.

Pencil on Paper
Airdrie, Alberta
Canada
www.pencilonpaper.ca

ISBN 978-1-9994820-2-2 (paperback)

ISBN 978-1-9994820-3-9 (ebook)

Cover design by Matt Seff Barnes

*For Kaleigh. Always.*

# ONE

Clint stood with his hands in his pockets, and his chin tucked to his chest. His green eyes, flecked with gray, focused on the clutch of plastic flowers near his feet. Placed by unseen hands, at least unseen by Clint, they reached up from windblown snow like jagged claws escaping a fresh grave. As the sun stretched its arms across the horizon, ushering in a new day, the reflection of the sky turned the crooked blooms a deep crimson.

Similar memorials appeared soon after the blockades came down, or maybe a little bit before, and the surviving residents of Niagara Country Village returned to see what remained of their homes, to process the scope of the tragedy they had experienced. Clint had not kept in touch with the others, not really, but the connection was one that could not easily be shaken.

While echoes of the storm drifted through Clint's memory, cool air billowed an old tarp caught on the burned remains of a single-story house to his left—one charred skeleton in a ring of seven others, with the shells of outbuildings, vehicles, and the frame of a camper littered among them. Happy memories of his time in the community that surfaced were soon overtaken—clouded by fire, smeared with blood. The weight of it dulled his senses to the point he did not hear footsteps in the snow until they were nearly on top of him.

He spun to face his truck. The stark beams of the headlights silhouetted a figure standing beside it, their features masked by shadows. The axe hanging from their right hand was clear enough, though. Clint's lips pinched tight as he pushed out a long breath and reached around his back to the gun clipped to his belt. "Can I help you?"

The person scratched the top of their head while sneaking a quick glance over their shoulder.

"Come on now, no need to be shy." Clint took hold of the handle, his fingers cold against the polymer grip. "Is there?"

The figure stepped forward into the halo cast by the headlights and tilted his head. "Clint?"

Clint scanned the man's face and did his best to imagine what it looked like in years past, without the frameless glasses over tired eyes, or the onset of gray hair at the temples. "Jacob? That you?"

Jacob nodded. A smile formed on his lips, but it cracked under the weight of their shared past.

"Jesus Christ." Clint drew his hand forward and up, pushing a strand of dirty-blond hair out of his face. "I was about ready to put a bullet in your brain."

"Oh. Sorry. I didn't recognize you at first. The beard and all."

Clint motioned to Jacob's hand. "I see your weapon of choice hasn't changed."

Jacob allowed a tentative look down and hefted the handle to adjust his grip. "I guess."

"You expectin' trouble?"

Jacob shrugged. "Can't be too careful, right?"

"Suppose so."

"That's what I figured, anyway. I mean, broken fence, fresh tracks." Jacob stepped forward and around Clint to stand on the other side of the memorial. "With everything else going on, I left the car by the road."

Clint nodded.

"You came for the anniversary too?"

"I don't know. Sort of."

Jacob stared off into the night. "To be honest, I haven't been back since. Guess I got a little nostalgic."

"Interestin' way to put it."

"Not sure that's the right word. Maybe I needed a reminder. We live in strange times."

A smile flickered at Clint's lips. "That we do."

"So…how've you been?"

Clint held out a hand and looked away. "Really, we don't need to—"

"I think we do, actually, after what we all went through."

"Yeah, well, maybe the thing to remember is, that was just the beginning."

Jacob nodded. "I was. And I'm sure a lot has happened since. Some I know about. Second hand, anyway."

Clint chewed on his lip while he held back the tremor in his jaw.

"We've been able to stay safe. For the most part. Except…" Jacob turned to the half-buried flowers. "Mati. She got stuck inside when they locked down Montreal. I…I haven't heard from her since."

"I'm sorry, man. I really am."

"They open the gates in two days. I want to be there

tonight, be as ready as I can." Jacob pinched his lips together after the bottom began to tremble. "I'll find her."

"It's a knack you two have. I don't doubt you will."

"Yeah." Jacob wiped at his nose. "So, what about you?"

Clint waited until the uncomfortable silence got to be too much. Jacob's calm eyes expressed his patience, his understanding.

Clint broke his gaze away again. "If you really want to know, everything's pretty fucked. Erica took the kids south after the last outbreak. Haven't seen them in person since. I'm sure you heard about everything that led up to it. Between quarantine blockades up north, and the restrictions at the border, my options are limited. Mostly, I'm told I don't have the right attitude or skillset to maintain employment in the current economy." He lowered his eyes, licked at his bottom lip. "It's come to the point I don't have anything left to stick around for."

"What are you going to do then?"

Clint looked up to receding darkness and tall clouds in the distance—a storm conserving its energy for another day. "Figured I'd head west, see how far I get. I hear they're usually looking for people to work the rigs in northern Alberta during migration season."

Jacob nodded. "I've heard it's not the easiest place to get into though."

Clint diverted his gaze. "Yeah, well, I'm gonna see what I can figure out." He wiped at his nose. "Just need to stay on for a season or two, then I can head to the coast, buy something that floats, and sail south until the butter melts. Maybe I won't have to deal with this shit virus after that."

"Sounds like a good enough plan."

"Guess I'll find out."

They stood in silence until Jacob turned, his free hand shielding his eyes against the rising sun. "Guess it's time to get moving."

Clint clawed his fingers down through his beard. "Yeah, suppose it is."

Jacob raised the axe and rested it over his shoulder. "Clint? Take care of yourself. Okay?"

Clint nodded, but his eyes stayed vacant. "You too, Jacob."

Jacob sighed and focused on Clint like he had more to say. Instead, he turned away from the man, once his neighbor, and in some ways his friend, and continued to his car without another word.

Clint stayed with his hands in his pockets until the whine of the car's engine faded in the distance. He gently shook his head to bring him out of his pondering, then sniffed and raised his face to the clear sky above him. Whether from the light, the chill in the air, or something else, moisture built in the corners of his eyes. He sat in the moment for as long as he could stand to, then cleared his throat, wiped at his cheeks, then got into his truck.

TWO

The highway slowed a few kilometers before Sudbury. Lines of semis and loaded trailers mixed with short- and long-distance commuters, all with a simple goal of getting to where they needed to be before the crossings closed.

Clint's leg vibrated as he eased the truck along. It should not have been so busy, not as late in the day as it was. The plan was to drive straight through to Thunder Bay, but he already knew that plan had changed. As he neared the last bend before the crossing, it was easier to see the volume of traffic being turned back or diverted into the city. Barriers along the roadway meant he had no other option than to wait it out.

After the five-ton box truck in front of him executed a sloppy three-point turn and accelerated south, Clint idled up to three crossing guards who were out on foot, performing preliminary checks. All wore full-body suits checkered with light-weight armor and sealed joints at the neck and wrists. The one with a tablet in is hand stepped closer. He only had a gun strapped to his belt. The lines around his eyes showed it had been a long day.

Clint rolled down his window and forced a tight smile. "Afternoon."

The pair with rifles fanned out and circled the truck. The guard with the tablet held it level with Clint's face and tapped at the screen. "Passport?"

"Am I getting across right now?"

"That all depends."

"Then what's the—"

The tablet radiated a satisfied tone, and a green checkmark lit the screen. The guard lowered it then held out a gloved hand. "Passport."

"Christ, okay." Clint leaned forward and pulled a small leather folder from the back pocket of his jeans. He flipped it open as he held it toward the guard. His driver's license showed behind the plastic window at the top. His inter-city passport showed in the bottom.

The guard looked from the documents to Clint, searching past the differences in the images. "Where are you heading today?"

"At this point, I'd settle for Sault St. Marie."

"Unfortunately, that won't be possible. There's been a breach in the fence a couple clicks before. Based on volume and delays because of the repair, the estimates place arrival well after sundown."

Clint glanced in his side mirror as one of the armed guards ran a hand along the box of his truck, craning their neck to better see inside. "Isn't that the whole point of the bloody fence, so we can still drive after dark?"

"We've had too many incidents. The Transportation Minister changed the curfew last week."

Clint held back his opinion on the matter. "What are my options, then?"

"Sudbury, or home, if you've got enough time."

"Can't afford to get a hotel."

"Then you'd best get to one of the secured overnight lots before they fill up."

Clint eyed the crossing and weighed his chances. Retractable metal columns and tire spikes were one thing. The sniper towers were another situation entirely. He pressed his foot harder on the brake and turned back to the guard. "When does the queue normally start?"

The guard motioned to the gates before scratching at his jaw. "The morning shift lets the early birds hang on around five-thirty or six."

"Okay then." Clint shifted the truck into gear. "That's when I'll be here."

———

Clint arrived at the crossing well before sunrise, but just in time to join the line of other vehicles anxious to head west. At the point of official sunrise, the crossing lit up, and the guards pushed vehicles through as fast as they could to ease the backlog.

With the morning sun glaring over the side of his face, Clint pressed the accelerator. Past the secondary gate, he merged into the fast lane and put his foot to the floor. The big V8 howled as the truck lurched forward. The tight mesh of the three-meter-tall security fence on either side of the highway blurred as he gained speed. He only let up to accommodate slower traffic, but it was not long before he was setting the pace with a group of three or four others, nothing but the open road ahead of them.

Cruising along, he lifted his hand over the steering wheel to better see the clock. Less than four hours to Sault St. Marie. Assuming no other breaches, and the weather held, it would be just under eight hours to Thunder Bay. The crossing west would likely be closed by the time he arrived, so that meant another night sleeping on the back seat, keeping one ear open in case someone tried to steal his gear. As long as he made it past Winnipeg before dark, more importantly, past the federally mandated containment fence, he knew he could relax. He could move freely, in whichever direction suited him, at his own pace. Also, lower populations meant the dangers of traveling at night were fewer.

# THREE

Passing through the Thunder Bay checkpoint happened later in the morning than Clint had hoped, but the road to Winnipeg was smooth and clear. After a quick pitstop, he left Winnipeg just as the shadows began to grow long. Instead of continuing on the Number 1, he diverted south to Highway 83.

Clint gripped the steering wheel tightly with both hands and stared straight ahead to the limits of the truck's headlights. Hours of unfamiliar roads passing by in the dark had eroded his sense of place and what little energy remained. Even so, he carried on, being close to his goal but not far enough away from the things he wanted to leave behind.

After a signpost confirming the turnoff for a village called Forget, Saskatchewan, Clint pulled off the highway. He sat straight and checked the rearview mirror, then out the side windows. With no other headlights in sight, he reached under the dash and flipped a switch, far enough back not to easily be seen, close enough he could reach it and still see to drive. The lights inside and outside the truck disappeared.

Plunged into the starlight din, Clint allowed his eyes a

moment to adjust, then slammed his foot down on the brake and cranked the steering wheel to the right. The truck leaned hard, bucked against the low shoulder, then evened out as it found a path down a narrow gravel road barely wide enough for two vehicles to pass each other.

Clint held his head low, focus jumping between the path forward and the truck's mirrors. He slowed to a reasonable pace once it became clear he had not been seen, or at least followed.

He veered toward the first right-hand turn and continued until a rare patch of trees filled in both sides of the road. Clint maneuvered the truck down and through until he was afforded some amount of cover. Leaning back in his seat, he shut the engine down and waited.

What he was waiting for never became apparent. Perhaps a certain number of stars through the cracks in the windshield, or when he could just see the wisps of his breath as the air cooled. Eventually, he unbuckled and stepped out into the dried grass and snow.

Around the back of the truck, he zipped his heavy canvas jacket to his neck, dropped the tailgate, and rooted deep into the mess of stacked boxes and bins to pull out a grease-stained grocery store tote bag. Watching all around, listening for any sign to indicate he was not alone, he sat the bag on the gate and spread the top open. Digging down to the bottom, he took out a faded Alberta license plate and a multi-bit screwdriver, then dropped them to the ground. Next, he shook out a black leather wallet, an ATM envelope, and a can of lighter fluid before tossing the bag off into the scrub. Clint tucked the wallet and envelope into his jacket pocket. He reached up along the side of the box to collect a folding shovel, then lifted the tailgate and pushed it to the first click of the latch.

Clint knelt, picked up the screwdriver, and turned out the three remaining screws holding the Ontario license plate to the bumper. ZMBHNTR. The plate and the truck were mementos of a life relegated to a dream, or one that belonged to someone else. The truck was found pretty much untouched the day after he brought Krystal home. Why he kept it, why he did not run it into a ditch and set it on fire, a physical embodiment of his life at that moment, he could not recall. After setting the Alberta plate in place, Clint put two screws in to secure it. At the front of the truck, he repeated the removal, then set both reminders of his previous life aside. He sighed and tilted his head back, pulled up the bottom hem of his jacket, undid his belt, and unzipped his pants.

The warm stream of urine wafted a dense, acrid haze. It washed down the clean patch on the front bumper, and a wide patch of ground in front of it. Once the stream ebbed, Clint put himself together, and out of habit looked over his shoulder. He stepped forward into the warm, damp ground and twisted the toe of his boot, then lifted it and smeared the resulting mess across the bumper like an amateur artist coaxing an image onto their canvas. When it had blended well enough with the existing grime and last summer's bug guts, he stood back and folded out the shovel.

The pointed tip chipped out a hasty divot in the cold ground big enough to accept the license plates, thin metal folded in half and stomped flat with the heel of his boot. Clint took out his old wallet from his back pocket, opened it to remove the thin stack of folded bills and a dogeared picture of his kids from inside, then stashed them in his back pocket. His Ontario license and passport, health care card, and registration dropped onto the license plates. Next, he took out the lighter fluid, and the chrome flip-top lighter that lived in his front pants pocket. He kneeled and shot two short spurts of fluid into the hole, then flipped the lighter and set the flame close.

After it caught, he stood and doused the hole with fluid. Fire and dark smoke billowed, accentuating deep lines around his haunted eyes. He watched and waited, adding more fluid if the flames threatened to fail at their task, until the cards and paper were specks, the wallet no more than a shriveled ball of char, and the license plates blackened and warped from the heat. Clint emptied the bottle overtop, then dropped it in as well. As the last of the flames diminished, he covered it all with the uprooted soil, then pushed dead grass and leaves overtop.

Clint opened the driver's side door, then remembered the envelope. He pulled it out and flipped the top open. The first item he removed was a sticker with a tractor being the main image with *No Farmers, No Food* in bold letters underneath. After peeling the paper backing, he smoothed it over the bottom corner of the truck's rear window. The next item he removed was a narrow plastic rectangle with its own backing to be peeled. Instead of the rear window, Clint stepped into the truck and leaned over the dash. With his forehead rubbing on the inside of the windshield, and with an unsteady hand, he positioned the new VIN tag in place. With that done, he sat behind the wheel and pushed out a long breath.

He swept empty and crumpled energy drink cans onto the passenger-side floor, then stared at the mess and what it covered. He laid out his new wallet like the cherished cargo that it was before reaching over to the passenger footwell for a bundled-up hoodie, still warm from resting beside the heater vent. He unzipped and shrugged off his jacket, slipped the hoodie over his head, then slid back into his jacket. Adjusting the hood over his collar, he stretched out his neck and shoulders to release tension, then started the truck and put it in gear.

Clint advanced slowly at first, turning the wheels into the symbolic grave of his old life, packing them down properly as some small form of ceremony. Up on the road, he straightened the wheel and put his foot down.

At the next intersection, well back from the crooked stop sign, he let the truck idle. Reaching under the dash, he flipped the switch to bring the truck's lights back, then felt around to confirm the burner phone he had stashed was still in place.

Clint rolled through Weyburn an hour later. From there he moved back to the Number 1 Highway and drove on in the slow lane, leaned forward in his seat with both hands tight on the wheel like the nervous driver that he was.

The median fence blurred as it passed. Clint lifted his eyes twice from the road as he sped along; once at the roadside camera past the Highway 614 turnoff, mounted low on a lamp post, camouflaged to look like and electrical access panel, and again two kilometers before the Maple Creek turnoff for the other roadside camera, a stark black box, tall on a black post, right out in the open.

A few minutes later he idled into Maple Creek and pulled through an empty gas station parking lot. He backed into a spot along the front of the convenience store and shut the engine down. He checked his mirror for the sign on the front of the building showing the stores hours, rubbed at his eyes to make them work better, then released a long breath and checked the clock on the dash. Three hours would have to be enough. He crossed his arms, leaned his head back, and drifted to sleep while the engine ticked and pinged as it cooled.

# FOUR

After the gas station manager tapped on the truck's window to wake him, Clint went inside to empty his bladder and stock up for the remainder of his trip. He shuffled to the till with his arms full of pre-packaged sandwiches, energy drinks in tall aluminum cans, and the biggest to-go cup of coffee available. He laid everything out, then dropped a stack of bills tall enough to cover the food and a full tank of gas. Within seconds of the pump clicking off, Clint pulled away from the gas station and pointed west.

As the truck droned on, Clint's road-weary eyes focused on a wide brown sign, perched between two heavy timbers, as it flashed past. The headlights cast warm light onto the signs lining the road. A small rectangle offered a faded and bullet-riddled *Welcome to Alberta*. The next, much larger and brightly lit so as not to be missed, *Keep Alberta Rat Free*. The rodent in question was the silhouetted form of an undead character, like something from a sixties B-movie, in the crosshairs of a rifle scope. His shoulders settled, but the tightness in his chest held on. Clint checked his speed, adjusted his rearview mirror, and continued forward.

The flashing lights came later than he expected them to, considering he had crossed one of the few uncontrolled sections of the border before the crack of dawn, and with rumors of predictive intelligence license plate scanning and algorithms flagging suspicious vehicles. The siren barely had time to sound before he was off the throttle and drifting to the shoulder. He put the truck in park, shut the engine down, then rested his hands on top of the steering wheel.

The officer stopped two arms-length from Clint's door. Since he didn't have a gun in his face, Clint assumed the stolen plate had worked, that the money he had paid to have the registry system unofficially updated had been well spent. He hoped his luck would continue to hold out, but he knew that more than one assumption a day was a great way to work yourself into a corner.

The officer faced Clint square on, the thumb of one hand tucked under the strap of his ballistic vest, APP emblazoned across the front, but no name badge to be seen. His other hand rested on the holster of what seemed to be a larger-than-normal service firearm. The officer's narrowed eyes scanned the cab of the truck and the box.

Though Clint did not think it wise to look behind him, a flash of movement in the passenger-side mirror hinted at the partner around back somewhere doing the same. It was only in that moment that he wondered if they decided to search, if they'd get far enough to the black duffle bag buried at the front of the box with his gun in it.

The officer locked onto Clint and lowered his hand from his vest. "Eyes open." He pulled a device similar to an old flip-phone from a pouch at his stomach, below a collection of ten-round magazines, and held it out.

A narrow red beam settled on Clint's forehead. It split and fanned out over his eyes, then vanished. As the officer studied the results, Clint studied the officer from the corner of his eye.

The Provincial Government replaced the Royal Canadian Mounted Police with the Alberta Provincial Police after the first wave of the infection reached the border. Kicked them out, more like it. It didn't take much to convince a population force-fed propaganda and protectionist ideals day in and day out. Concerns over the militaristic nature of the force, both in uniform and in attitude, along with alleged abuses of power, were easy to suppress in a world where legitimate news was created by anyone with a social media handle.

"License, registration, and passport." The officer folded and secured the scan device and held out a waiting hand.

Clint looked forward. His gaze flicked to the rearview mirror out of habit. The officer's partner, long gun raised to their shoulder and a mask over the lower half of their face, hovered around the back corner of the truck. Clint locked his eyes on the blank slate that was the road ahead. He slowly lifted his left hand from the steering wheel and clawed the requested documents from the dash, passed them out the window, then set his hand back on the wheel.

The officer flipped through the cards, front and back, focus shifting between the information and Clint's face. "Heading home?"

"That's the plan."

"Fort Macleod?"

"Yes, sir."

"What took you out of province?"

Clint motioned behind him. "Uncle in Weyburn kicked it. No other family to speak of, so I went to clean his place out."

The officer held out Clint's documents, then stepped up onto the truck's front tire. He shone the beam of his flashlight on the base of the windshield, paused for a moment, then hopped down and clicked the flashlight off. "Why the late-night run?"

"Had yesterday off but have to work today. Did what I had to do."

"What do you do for work?"

Clint flexed his fingers, raising cracked and grease-stained nails. "Heavy-duty mechanic."

"Did you go any further than Weyburn?"

The underlying question, of course, had he gone as far as Manitoba? Had he crossed the containment fence?

"Straight there, straight back."

"Why didn't you take the number one?"

Clint shrugged as he dropped his papers on the seat next to him. "Slow movin' wide load at Maple Creek. Prefer the quiet roads anyhow."

The officer looked over the bed of the truck one last time, nodded, stepped back. "I won't keep you any longer." He smiled like it was practiced. "Be careful out there."

Clint nodded. "Will do."

As he turned the ignition to start the engine, he watched the officers walk back to their cruiser and sit behind the wheel. The red-and-blue flashing lights extinguished, plunging everything except the world immediately in front of them back into darkness, then Clint pulled away.

Through dust kicked up by the truck's tires grasping for purchase on the gravel, he kept a close eye on the mirrors, watching until the cruiser's headlights disappeared in the distance. Clint focused forward and took his first full breath since crossing the provincial border.

He drove on, through Medicine Hat, then south on the Number 3 Highway. More than a few times, the glow of headlights flared in the rearview. Though he couldn't see, he expected that a black cruiser would be behind them, and that at any moment, the flashing lights would return. He did his best to keep to himself, made no erratic maneuvers, and moved in the direction he told the APP he was moving. At Taber, he pulled off at a gas bar, filled the tank for good measure, then parked facing the highway.

He sat and watched the flow. Regular people going about their day. The morning rush, such as it was in a small town, had eased into normalcy. Normal was a perspective, though. It was a version of normal that Clint had not known for years. The lack of fences and checkpoints raised his anxiety more than he thought it would.

While fighting the urge to close his eyes, Clint checked back and forth along the highway, searching for anything out of place. Grazing past the rearview, his eyes glimpsed what could have been an APP cruiser behind him. He blinked twice and looked again. Just an old lady, probably heading home after coffee with the girls.

Clint gripped the wheel with one hand, and with the other, absent-mindedly reached to his shirt pocket for a package of cigarettes that wasn't there. His upper lip curled, and he cursed the habit thought forgotten. He pulled out of the parking lot and focused back on the road, waited for a gap, then shot north across the highway.

All he could think about was that he told the APP officer he was heading west. He fought so many times to keep his foot from sinking to the floor, that he eventually set the cruise control, and then leaned back, chewing the nail on his tremoring hand.

Three hours later, Clint arrived at the Number 9 Highway. His escape plan had only been developed so far, like a book half-outlined, and his next decision would push him into the unknown. He idled at the intersection, mind spinning, while some sort of direction attempted to form in his mind. Soon after, a semi with twin tanker trailers flew across his vision, shaking him out of his daze. Clint drew in a deep breath, cranked the steering wheel to the right, and pressed down on the accelerator.

He stopped next in Youngstown, a small village just off the highway. After loading up enough food to cover lunch and dinner, and filling the truck with fuel, he was back on the road. At Highway 884 he diverted north, then drove on for hours with sugary caffeine drinks and blaring music keeping his eyes open. He drove east when the journey demanded, but otherwise kept his bearing.

Before passing through Bonnyville, Clint noticed a change in the landscape. Soft hills rose up, replacing the flat roads that had given little of interest to focus on. Poplar trees and dark evergreens framing the two-lane highway grew taller and huddled in denser clusters. As he passed by turnoffs for the small towns scattered along the route, their names forgotten before he arrived at the next, he offered fleeting glances to signs for small businesses he had not considered a need for, patches of frozen marshes, and roadside graveyards with a handful of plain headstones contained within low, cast-iron fences. Before reaching Cold Lake, he passed a chipped and faded sign with *Respect Our Land* in red, block letters, nearly eclipsed by a taller sign in front with flashy graphics and details of the past summer's air show.

Clint entered Cold Lake from the west and soon arrived at the marina. He sat idling, watching the great expanse of flat white in front of him. With no major roads in sight, he drove south. He kept his head low as he went through town and passed the entrance to the air base, only relaxing once the matching sailboat centurions at the city limits were in his rearview.

He continued south until he confirmed he was alone on the highway, then pulled off onto a secondary road. As the sun set and the air cooled around him, he kept going, turning on a whim. All the while, the path ahead got smaller and rougher. After being bounced around for a few kilometers, he pulled the truck into a tight cluster of birch trees and shut the engine down.

Surrounded by bare branches and trunks flaking white bark, he raised his eyes to the sky. He sat in awe, scanning the vast array of stars above, most he was sure he had not seen before in his life. As his gaze twitched across countless constellations, his lids became too heavy to keep open. With that, Clint leaned into his hands, still wrapped over the steering wheel, then released a long breath and closed his eyes.

# FIVE

Brandon stretched out on his unmade bed, shirtless, jeans unbuttoned, and socks festering on the floor beside him. His ghost-white feet were crossed. One arm, slight but muscular, tucked under his head with his fingers grazing the stubble of his reddish -brown hair. His other hand propped up an e-reader with a black-and-white screen on his chest. His eyes scanned line by line, even as the door to his room creaked open.

"Hey, old man."

Brandon advanced the page with the tap of his thumb. "Do I need to remind you, yet again, that you're older than I am? Or that I only just turned twenty-nine?"

"Age is state of mind, and yours should have retired already."

Brandon fought the smile pulling at his lips. "What's good, Perry?"

Perry scanned the empty walls of the eight-by-eight room. The desk, like something out of a high school classroom. The window barely big enough for a grown man to fit through, should he be so inclined. The single dome on the ceiling casting sharp light over all of it. Everything tagged with *Property of Ravenbak Energy Inc.* "Just gettin' ready to head into town. Wanted to see if you'd like to join."

"You all done for a bit?"

Perry let a sly smile creep across his face as he rubbed his nose with the back of his hand. "Yup. Lookin' forward to getting the hell out of here for a few days."

Brandon nodded. "Lucky."

"Lucky?"

Brandon tapped the screen again.

"I'm assuming that means you still got time to put in?"

"I've got a couple days to myself, but I said I'd stay on for another tour."

"What for?"

"Should be enough."

"Enough for what?"

Brandon lifted his head, drew his hand down to scratch the rough linework of the New Brunswick flag over his heart, the one hastily applied late one drunken night to cover the initials of a love gone bad. "To get me home. You know, for more than a week."

"Really? You gonna do it?"

"That's the plan."

"Finally gonna live out your dreams as a potato inspector?"

Brandon allowed a smile to form. "Could be."

"Your parents know you're comin'?"

Brandon shook his head.

"What about…"

Brandon looked to Perry for the first time. "Just the government."

Perry snorted. "Crazy that you have to apply to get back into the place you were born, but I guess that's the world we live in." Perry checked over his shoulder. "Well, I'm assuming that means you're set on doin' old man things. Enjoy your night, then." Perry turned to go but stopped. "Hey, you seen Connor?"

"Not since yesterday. He was paying too much attention to what the new guy was doing, and a pipe nearly took his head off."

"For real?"

"Said he was okay but haven't heard anything since he went to get checked over."

"Shit."

"Yeah."

Perry tapped the door frame. "All right. Take it easy."

"You too, Perry."

# SIX

Clint woke to a weathered face with pale eyes pressed up against the passenger-side window of the truck, one crooked hand held to shield their view. He didn't have the energy to be surprised, so leaned back in his seat, ran his hands over his face and through his beard to massage some life into himself, then turned the ignition enough to roll the window down.

"Mornin'."

"Mornin'?" The man leaned a forearm against the door. The silver mustache that all but covered his lips eased up on one end. "It's gone half past eight in the evenin'. Near abouts anyway."

"Oh." Clint held his wrist up to his face out of habit, but he had trouble making out the numbers on his watch in the dim light, so instead pushed the hood of his sweater away from his face and craned his neck to search the darkness. "Shit."

"Might be the word for it." The man pushed up on the sweat-stained ivory cowboy hat atop his head. While thin in the face, the man was a little sturdier than Clint was used to seeing. He had a set to his eyes that was better able to see the land and how to exist with it. One most people had lost. "You workin' off a drunk?"

Clint yawned and shook his head.

"You ain't one a them tweakers, is ya?"

A smile almost caught on Clint's lips. "No, sir. Too many hours behind the wheel is all."

The man scanned the mud and road grime along the side of the truck. "You long haulin'?"

"Somethin' like that."

"Ain't nothin' wrong with drivin' truck if it means your family is fed."

"No, sir."

"You anywhere near home?"

Clint didn't respond with the obvious answer, since home was a concept that he was not sure he understood in that moment. "No, sir."

The man searched Clint's face. "Well, figure you should get on out of here either way, 'fore the cherries and berries come snoopin'."

"Wouldn't want that."

"No, sir, you wouldn't." The man eyed Clint a moment, then peeled off a battered leather glove and reached up through the window. "Jack Engehart."

Clint leaned over and took the offered hand, attempted to meet it grip for grip. "Clint."

Jack nodded. "Good meetin' ya." He slipped his glove back on and stepped back.

That was when Clint saw the rifle tucked under his arm.

Jack focused on his boots and repositioned, so he pointed toward the road. "Back your rig up out of here. Follow my lead. The ranch ain't more than a couple miles back. It'll give you a place to sort yourself out. I drive slow, so you won't get lost."

"Appreciate it, Jack."

Clint watched as Jack made careful progress to an old Dodge long-box idling at the edge of the road. After he swallowed to unstick his tongue from the roof of his mouth, he reached across the seat to the pile of cans and food packaging next to him. Finding everything empty, he simply waited for Jack to pull ahead, then he started the engine and shifted into reverse.

———

Clint drove on autopilot, not looking further than the headlight glow on Jack's tailgate. After turning from the rough gravel road, rumbling over a rust-colored cattle guard, and through a pair of heavy metal gates that were staked open, they continued along what was little more than two worn ruts in the ground. It was then that Clint raised his eyes. The path led them from a scrub field and dropped them down into a grove of thin, leafless trees. Rocking back and forth over uneven ground, they crested a wide bend before the path opened into flat land flecked with dead grass and low shrubs. Dried up watering holes scattered out like a mosaic. Small groups of stout, black cattle stood watch as the trucks lumbered past.

The old Dodge pulled around a line of parked cars and a beat-up old wrecker truck with a phone number laid out in hastily applied stick-on numbers, then up in front of a squat, two-story house with a lean-to garage on the right-hand side. Clint parked next to it but left the engine running. Jack came around the back of his truck, hiking his pants. He motioned across the yard, along a rutted path that carried on past a small, open-front shed, and a barn with a domed wood shake roof, and peeling red paint that had faded to brown. "Park yourself out back of the big shop. Fit in with the junkyard if you can." He hooked a thumb over his shoulder. "I'll get the coffee started."

Clint nodded and shifted into reverse. He idled through the yard and a break in the fence that sectioned off the front of the property, past a line of tractors in various states of disrepair, and between large, tilled garden beds with weathered timber fences wrapped around them.

The shop turned out to be a giant, windowless white box with a closed roll-up door on the end that could have easily allowed two grain trucks side by side. A rusted pot-belly stove stood in tall, dead grass a few steps from the only visible man-door. Otherwise, the front perimeter was clear. As Clint rounded the back of the shop, that situation changed. Old pickups, some missing their box, some missing fenders, lined half the span of the back wall. Tucked in and among stacks of rough-cut timbers, the cab from an old combine, a flat trailer, up on blocks, heaped with old washing machines and rolls of plastic snow fence.

He eased the truck over the uneven ground to an open spot, barely wide enough, and backed in, leaving room to drop the tailgate. After squeezing out of the driver's door, he locked the truck and stashed his keys. Clint moved to open ground, stuffed his hands in his pockets, then scanned the high cloud cover lit by the moon and the western fields beyond. A glint of light through the crooked trees marking the edge of the yard caught his attention. Beyond, the darkness took all sight, so he decided to leave what hid in it a mystery, grabbed his things, and headed to the house.

———

Clint waited outside the front door of the ranch house with a pack strung over his shoulder and his hat in his hands. A flat piece of driftwood mounted above the door had what he assumed was the ranch brand burned into it, an E on its side next to the numeral four, both perched above a quarter circle. A knot in the wood looked like an eye, and Clint could not help but wonder if it was watching him. When the door finally creaked open, Jack nodded and ushered him in. "Don't worry 'bout your boots."

Clint followed through the entryway, scraping his feet on the heavy fiber mat inside the door, past a line of jackets and Jack's hat hung on a piecework menagerie of hooks. He took only a cursory glance to his left, to a cluster of family photos on the wall beside the telephone, the largest being of Jack looking younger than he did now, holding hands with a woman with a warm smile and platinum hair, then through the opening to a living area with wood-trimmed, floral-print couches facing each other, and an upright piano at the far end, before moving further into the kitchen.

Clint sat last at the long table, where a plain white mug, filled to the brim with black coffee, waited for him. He took off his hat and set it over his knee. The chair was next to Jack, who sat at the far end, and across from a woman with a mug of her own. Her back was straight and tall. One short, painted nail clicked the ceramic side. Her dark-brown hair was pulled back into a no-nonsense ponytail that ended just above her shoulders. Amber eyes locked onto Clint like a prison guard watching an inmate leaving their cell.

Jack moved a glass ashtray piled with crinkled butts out of the way, blew at the steam over his cup, then took a sip that reverberated around the room. "Clint, this is my daughter, Christina."

Clint nodded to Christina. "Good to meet you."

She nodded back.

"She helps me run the ranch, such as it is these days."

Christina's grip tightened around her mug. "Part of that means I vet all his strays."

Clint nodded again, unsure how else to respond.

"Strays isn't as derogatory a term as you'd think. Not everybody fits in everywhere. Me, I don't care what you look like, where ya from, or who ya used to be. Don't hurt nobody, and pull your weight, then you're welcome to stay. Maybe that makes me progressive by today's standards but seems to me it's just takin' care of each other, like we're supposed to."

Jack focused out the window. "In my grandfather's time, we owned as far as the eye could see. There was cattle as far as the eye could see. Life doesn't get easier though, doesn't get less expensive either, what with corporations' takin' everything over. Conglomerates. We're down to a quarter section and eighty or a hundred head dependin' on the season. It's enough." Jack sipped from his mug, stared at it after it was set back on the table. "For now, at least."

The kitchen thundered with three heavy staccato impacts to the front door. Jack and Christina straightened and locked eyes. Clint's whole body tightened, as did his grip on the edge of the table.

Christina put her hands flat to push back and stand.

Jack waved her off. "Sit." He let out a long sigh as he got up and shuffled to the front door.

Clint sat perfectly still, heart pounding in his ears.

Christina held a finger to her lips.

The front door creaked open. Jack cleared his throat. "Yes, sir. What can I do for you?"

A voice came gruff, with false pleasantry. "Hello Jack. How are things?"

"You know, doin' what we can with what we've got."

"That's good to hear, I suppose." A beep echoed from a two-way radio, followed by mumbled chatter. "Listen, I apologize for bothering you so late in the day, but I'm curious if you've seen any vehicles around that seem out of place?"

"Out of place in what way?"

"Oh, I don't know, like maybe you haven't seen them around before."

"Nothin' I can recall."

"You out this evening checking the herd?"

"I was."

"You moved them to the south pasture last week, right?"

Jack hesitated. "Yes, sir."

"We had a call about a truck parked off in the trees. Just want to make sure nothing funny is going on. We're here to look out for you, Jack." A pause. "You, and your family."

A forced chuckle. "You know we appreciate it, Sergeant Spannhake, we do, but ain't nobody been around but the neighbors, as far as I been told." Jack snuck a glance over his shoulder, not to the kitchen, but to the shotgun tucked under the jacket closest to the corner of the foyer. "And we tend to take care of ourselves just fine."

"I know you do, Jack, I know you do." Radio chatter called out once more, Spannhake responded in a low voice, then came another pause. "Oh, Jack, any chance those Wingrove boys are around here somewhere?"

Jack straightened. "Will be soon if they ain't already."

Spannhake nodded. "Tell Odell I said hello. When you see

him, of course." He glanced over his shoulder. "Well, I hope you have a pleasant rest of your day. Be sure to reach out if you see anything."

"Will do."

The door eased closed and latched.

Jack came into the kitchen, hands in his pockets, eyebrows high but gaze low. He stopped behind his chair but didn't sit.

Clint watched and waited.

Jack pushed out a long breath and scratched at the wiry hair at his temple. "Anyway,"—he looked to Clint—"guess with that sort of attention bein' paid so soon, we need to get down to it."

Clint waited out the pause as long as he could. He leaned back. "What is it we need to get down to, Jack?"

Jack bent forward and set his hands on the top of his chair. "I'm gonna assume you have reasons to avoid the kind of attention our friend there is offerin'."

Clint swallowed. "Fair assumption."

"You done anythin' that's gonna bring trouble? You hurt anyone?"

Clint looked from Jack to Christina's hard gaze. Too many people to count. People he loved, most notably. "Not in any way the law'd care about."

"I take it by you sleepin' in the trees that you ain't really from around here."

"No, sir."

Clint flinched when Christina spoke. "Where are you from?"

The carefully crafted script built in his throat. He opened his mouth to let it but was interrupted.

"We don't have time for the bullshit answer."

Clint started to smile, but it broke under the weight he had carried for the last few days, months, and years. He wrapped a hand around his coffee but didn't lift it. "Ontario."

Christina sat straight, eyes wide. "Where?"

"Does it really matter?"

"To me it does."

Clint cleared his throat. "If you're asking how close I was to the whole mess, closer than anyone should have been."

Christina opened her mouth to continue her line of questioning, but Jack held out a hand. "You lost people then?"

Clint's lips pinched and his jaw squared. "I lost everyone. One way or another."

Christina looked to her father, crossed her arms, and sat back in her chair.

Jack nodded. "Seems about the only place someone'd come from that'd make old 'Berta look good, I'll give you that." He side-eyed Clint. "Pardon the inquiry, but it bears askin'. You ain't sick?"

Clint shook his head. "I've avoided it so far. Somehow." Clint stared at his hands. He continued on out of habit. "Vaccinated, and all that."

A smile tugged at Jack's lips and his unkempt brows raised. "I try not to have an opinion, but as a general piece of advice, might want to keep that to yourself for the most part. It's joined religion and politics as somethin' you don't discuss at family gatherin's."

"Noted."

"Outside of that, where you headed to?"

"Not sure."

Jack locked eyes with his daughter. Clint understood a conversation was taking place, some sort of genetic telepathy trained into them, but he had no idea what was being discussed until Jack turned back to him.

"You'd be welcome to join us here if you like."

Christina cleared her throat.

Jack's smile wavered. "On probation'ry terms, of course."

"Understood."

"The expectation is you contribute. Take care of your space. Take care of the person workin' next to you." Jack eyed Clint up and down. "You ever work a ranch?"

"No, sir." It took Clint a moment to catch on that he should continue. "I mean, I ain't afraid of hard work. Mechanically inclined and all that. Traditionally, my dealings with food-source animals have been through a rifle scope though."

Jack's smile flared. "A hunter. Long time?"

"Dad first took me out when I was eight."

"It's good to start young."

Clint gave an uneasy smile and stared at his hands. "At the time I was more interested in video games than spendin' my day in a cramped, frozen tent while Dad drank, but it is what it is."

"Sometimes the learnin' ain't easy. Bein' able to handle a rifle, provide for your family, that's no small thing."

Clint's trigger finger flexed. "Yes, sir."

Jack reached out for his coffee and drained it. "Well, it's been a long day, what say we get you settled in?"

Clint nodded and pushed back from the table. "Sounds good."

Jack held a hand to the room. "We've got a proper setup out in the shop, but you're welcome to use the facilities here until we can get you—"

Christina cut in. "Upstairs is off limits."

Jack nodded and lowered his eyes. "Upstairs *is* off limits. Family-only space, for the sake of it."

Clint swallowed. "Understandable."

Jack pushed his chair back and eased himself to standing. "Let's head out, then."

Without a word, Clint followed Jack into the yard with his pack over his shoulder.

Jack veered close to the front corner of the old barn. To the right was a woodshed with the doors pinned open. To the right of that was a large, galvanized fuel tank up on stilts, with a much newer looking gas hose and filler nozzle looped and hanging from the front. Another small shed capped off the row and marked where the yard ended and the pasture began.

Jack stopped in front of the barn and faced Clint. "It's near a hundred years old. The last of the original homestead. Still hangin' on." Jack eyed the skewed corners of the big door's frame. "Mostly, anyhow." Jack walked on. "She's off limits, though. Too dangerous at the moment."

Clint eyed the chain on the main door, the boarded-up windows, but also the footprints leading to and from the entrance, so kept any questions he had to himself.

They walked around the open-front shed, packed with a ride-on mower and an ATV, spools of barbed-wire and a stack of worn-out tires, then followed the patchy dirt road through the break in the fence that separated the main yard from the back. They kept to the right when the road forked, away from the parked tractors, and on toward the front of a modern barn.

"This here we put up a year or so back. I ain't one to disregard history, but everyone was happy when it was done." Under the glare of the sodium light mounted above, Jack pulled the big sliding door open part way and stepped to the side.

Clint slowed his breath and leaned in for a look as warm, musty air washed over him. In the shadows, along one side, two muscled forms shifted. They watched him with bulbous dark eyes. Cautious shuffling came from the other side.

"Eight bays. Two horses left. The rest is for the chickens, rabbits, and goats now." Jack pointed to the left corner. "Pens outside when the weather allows." Jack motioned to a narrow staircase with a severe angle rising to a square opening above them. "It also serves as temp'rary accommodations. Don't worry too much. It's clean and comfortable, all things considered. Cats do a good job of keepin' the mice out. Toilets are in the shop, but like I mentioned, the house is available, if you prefer."

Clint scratched under the edge of his hat. "Not the worst place I've laid my head down, I suppose."

Jack nodded. "I'm sure not."

Clint held the back of his hand over his mouth as he yawned.

Jack checked his watch. "It is about that time, isn't it."

"Yeah. Still have a bit of catchin' up to do on top of it all."

Jack smiled and motioned up the stairs. "All right then, have at it. Breakfast'll be at seven. We like to get an early start round here. You can meet the rest of the crew then."

Clint eyed the narrow passage and the dim light beyond. "Sounds good. Thanks, Jack."

# SEVEN

Clint stood at the bottom of the walkway leading to Krystal's front door. It was early, or late. In that moment it was hard to tell. A light breeze picked at the warmth in his cheeks and his nose. Tiny flecks of snow collected on his eyebrows and in his beard.

His gaze trailed from the porch, down the steps, along the fresh layer of snow, so far untouched. He studied the toes of his boots, the leather soaked through and dark, the laces loose after being hastily tied. His focus moved to his hand and the hunting knife he held with swollen fingers. A drop of blood released from the darkened tip fell to sully the pure white below. Clint wanted to let go of the knife, to be separate from it, throw it far away, but his fingers would not release. It was as if someone had played a cruel joke with a tube of superglue or that it would have been the same as releasing an arm, or his heart.

When he looked up, Krystal's front door was open a crack, but beyond it was darkness.

Dragging footprints marred the snow covering the porch. One set in, one set out.

Clint clenched his jaw as he turned to see where they might lead. Krystal's car idled at the curb, nobody in the passenger seat, nobody behind the wheel. Those facts didn't stop the engine from revving, and the front wheels turning to pull out into the street. A wisp of exhaust trailed as it drove away.

Clint lowered his head and raised his hand. Instead of the knife, his fingers grasped a carton of milk. The word 'missing' blazed across the top in a bold font, a black-and-white picture of Krystal positioned below. One of her eyes was swollen shut. Scratches at her temple. Blood seeped from her nose.

As Clint blinked tears away, and his grip tightened around the carton, he focused on the sidewalk at his feet. The covering of snow had been trampled to resemble the surface of an alien planet, the middle packed and pulverized, washed red. He traced the valley from the east to the west. The trail widened. The scar deepened. His eyes settled on a thin crack of light along the western horizon. Not as late as it could have been then, but an ending all the same.

# EIGHT

Clint shot upright and cried out. Across the loft, a barn cat jumped in shock and bolted away. Clint scanned each corner of the space as he held the heels of his hands against the pounding pressure at his temples. The two double mattresses closest to the stairs were untouched, clad in plain bedding with a plastic sheet tucked over to protect them. Each had a mismatched wooden kitchen chair beside to act as a nightstand. The papered rafters showed pink insulation where it had torn in spots. Dusty spiderwebs decorated the farthest corners and the small, clouded windows set into each end of the space. When his beating heart and erratic breath began to settle, Clint leaned forward, knees up, and ran his hands over his face.

"Fuck."

He blinked into the dim light cast by three yellow incandescent bulbs along the roof's peak and reached out to the wood chair beside his own bed to take his watch. He was late for breakfast. Standing on the creaking wood plank floor, he cleared his throat, then stalked off, making his way out of the barn and through the rolling fog toward the ranch house.

Clint knocked on the front door then glanced to the gate at the road out, and the heavy chain and lock holding it closed. After someone called out to come in, he did. He scraped his boots on the mat inside, then stopped at the entryway to the kitchen.

Seated at the head of the table with a coffee cup in front of him, Jack waved Clint in. "It's a little crazy in here at the moment, full house on account'a your arrival."

Clint nodded, the red flaring in his cheeks hardly noticeable underneath the already chilled skin. He unzipped his jacket but stayed in place. "Sorry, I was hoping to get cleaned up before breakfast."

Jack waved the thought away. "You're fine. Sit."

Clint nodded, then took the empty chair closest to him, the one at the opposite end of the table from Jack.

Clint counted four chairs on either side. His eyes flickered between the empty plate in front of him and the faces turned his way, some smiling, one most notably not. The man at Jack's right hand, broad in the shoulders and about Clint's age, but with long, black hair. He had one eye filled with broken red blood vessels, and a set of compact earbuds that were a close match to his deep skin tone. Clint was not sure he wanted to know too much about the big man, as if the knowledge itself might put him in danger.

"Everyone, this here's Clint. It's lookin' like he'll be hangin' around for a while." Jack pointed to the line of plates and bowls askew along the middle of the table. "Go on and dish up. Introductions can be done while you eat."

Clint nodded. He hesitated before reaching out for a colorful bowl with a scattering of fried potatoes and onions around the bottom. His stomach grumbled, a warning sign of how long it had been since he had a proper meal.

Jack looked to his left as Christina rounded the table. "You'n the boss're already acquainted, as far as these things go."

Christina leaned past Clint to drop a small plate of fried eggs in front of him, then held out a steaming coffee pot in her hand. "Something like that." She filled his cup to the brim, then turned away to top up the cups of the others.

Jack motioned to the tucked-in chair beside where Christina had been sitting. "That there would have been Grandson if you was on time." Jack held up a hand. "Not that I'm commentin' on that specifically. He left to catch his bus to school a few minutes before you arrived. Graduates high school next year. Still workin' out what comes next. Was in cadets for the longest time but decided it didn't align anymore. He's got some good things headed his way, don't worry 'bout that. Smart kid. We're all very proud." Jack nodded to the next in line. "This here is Patch and Andie. I'll leave the proper introductions to them."

The couple beside Clint looked like someone's grandparents from an old sitcom. Silver hair, thick glasses, wide smiles. They held hands on top of the table. The husband raised his free hand with a slight tremor and ran it over his side-part. "I'm Patch, this is my wife Andie. We've known Jack and the family going on forty years now, I guess. We moved onto the property a little while back after our own handful of acres became too much to hold on to. We like to take care of the horses and the other animals generally. My father raised horses most of his life, and Andie worked as a veterinary assistant before the kids came along, so it's a good fit for us." Patch adjusted his glasses on his round nose. "Oh,

I'm a retired electrical engineer, so help out with a few other things around here as well."

Clint raised his eyes to Jack. "Didn't realize farms need electrical engineers to run."

Jack put the flat of his hand on the table and gave a sly smile. "We'll get to that, don't you worry."

Clint swallowed and nodded to Patch and Andie. "Good to meet you." He filled his fork and continued eating.

Andie squinted her pale-blue eyes and leaned into her smile. "It's very nice to meet you as well."

The man to Clint's left held his cup in his hands and offered a tight smile but kept his wide-set eyes in front of him. The term pudgy would have been used if he was younger. His brown hair was wiry, unkempt. "I'm Duncan." He pointed a thumb to his left. "Odell's brother."

Clint held the back of his hand to his face as he chewed a mouthful of potatoes and bacon and gave Duncan a nod.

Jack leaned forward and motioned to Clint. "That's only part of it. Duncan here is ex-Airforce. We're all very grateful to have him. And his brother, of course."

Odell angled toward Clint, leaned with one arm propped over the back of his chair, but his belly still rested against the table. He could have been Duncan's twin, but in a picture from the future. Same wiry hair, but a little thinner, same round face, but a little heavier at the jowls. Odell nodded and picked at his teeth with his tongue. "I assume my reputation precedes me?"

Clint held his eye contact. "I'm afraid it hasn't."

"That's a shame." Odell smiled in a crooked way. "As mentioned, I'm Odell. You could say I'm the head of procurement for this here operation. Where there's demand, I am the supply."

Andie snickered. "Sometimes when there isn't any demand as well."

Happy murmurs circulated. Odell's expression soured but still held the hint of a sly grin, then he drained his coffee cup and sat straight on in his chair.

The chair next to Odell was tucked tight into the table. That left the big man on the end, seated beside Jack. He folded his napkin into a rectangle, placed it next to his plate, then straightened the fork beside it. He didn't look up or speak.

Breaking the silence, Jack cleared his throat. "This here's Porter. Bit of the strong, silent type. Good at keeping up at the day to day, good at the heavy liftin' and such. Management role, you could say, but in the hands-on way."

Clint glanced across from Porter as Christina took her seat. A stray thought about the nature of the big man's hands-on involvement drifted past, but he quickly pushed it away. Taking Porter's lead, Clint focused on his plate, dragged another fried egg over and mixed it up with what was left of the potatoes.

Jack drew from his coffee, then diverted the conversation. "Anyone have anything special on the go for today?"

Odell leaned back in his chair. "Got a run to make early this afternoon in case anyone needs supplies from town."

"I thought you normally make your runs on Friday?"

Odell scowled. "Heard there's a convoy hauling supplies into the base to fill up the new hangars and barracks. Tomorrow won't be nothin' but roadblocks and detours, which I ain't got time for."

Clint raised an eyebrow. "The base?"

Odell gave Clint a hard look, like an alien lifeform that had just walked into the room. "The base. You know, the fighter planes that are the foundation of our limited national security force?"

"Right. Sorry." Clint sunk his head further into his shoulders. "Still waking up, I guess."

Patch leaned forward on his forearms. "I wonder if they have trouble finding drivers for that kind of thing. I heard you're not even allowed on base unless you've got your vax card up to date."

Odell leaned back in his chair. "Good thing the reach of our illustrious federal government only makes it as far as the front gate. That's what I think."

Duncan shrugged. "Could be worse. Look at the shit show out east."

"Half of that's just overblown by the media. Keeps the herd in check."

Andie crossed her arms. "You think locking cities down is overblown? Like it's not actually happening?"

"It's only happening because of the government agenda. Besides, heard that Montreal is opening back up. How bad could it have been?"

Clint kept his eyes low, shoveled more food while his mind reeled with the possibilities. A sudden concern for Jacob emerged, which he had not expected.

Patch scraped a fork along his plate. "It used to be said you shouldn't believe anything you read and only half of what you see. Who knew that would only get worse as time went on?"

"You can believe it if you know where to look." Odell scowled and rolled his eyes to the ceiling. "Not my fault the goddamned Libtard—"

"*Enough.*" Jack wagged a finger around the group. "You

know politics ain't welcome at the table. Save yer bitchin' for your own time."

"Sorry, boss…" Odell focused on his plate.

"Ain't nothin' black and white in life. And it's import'nt to know what's fact and what's opinion." Jack set his jaw to one side. "We're more alike than not, which is why everyone bein' so divided these days confuses me." He side-eyed Christina, then sighed and motioned to Clint's plate. "Listen, don't mean to rush, but why don't we finish up here, then we can get on with the ten-cent tour before we start our day?"

Clint nodded, pushed his plate and what remained of his breakfast forward. Andie was soon there to collect the leftovers. She offered a nervous smile. "For the cats."

Clint nodded. "Of course, help yourself." He then stood and followed Jack out the front door.

Jack stopped just off from the porch and finished pulling his gloves on. "I figure I'll take ya out when I check the cattle later on, show you more of the place, but for now, we'll stick a little closer to home." Jack raised a hand toward the fields. "Technically, this is all First Nation land. But I guess everything is, in the end. Grandson will be fifth generation to work it, if he so chooses." Jack walked on. "People tend to keep to themselves after the last few years. We ain't no different, I suppose. Hell, what I'm saying is, not that you'd expect to find a concern, but stay on the property until you get a better feel for things.

"Noted."

They walked through the break in the fence, but instead of heading right to the barn as they had the night before, they followed Clint's tire tracks past the garden beds and went toward the halo cast by the lights on the big shop.

"The growin' season ain't much here, of course, but we

generally have enough to keep everyone from starvin' without too many trips to the grocery or feed store." Jack looked back over his shoulder to the two opaque-paneled greenhouses on the north-east side of the new barn. "Like I said, we try to be self-sufficient, make the old ways work. What we can't do on our own, we got like-minded friends in the area that can." At the shop, he opened the small door, reached in to flip a light switch, then stepped aside. "In here's another situation though."

Clint shielded his eyes as he stepped through into crisp light. The tang of electricity hummed in the air. The space in front of the big roll-up door was empty, save for the darkened strips left by trucks pulling in and out over the concrete. The near-side wall held long steel workbenches covered with power tools, welders, an engine hoist. Square polyethylene tanks in galvanized cages with skid bases stacked three high, a menagerie of electrical panels and gauges with flashing light displays, and banks of batteries lined the wall across from them.

Tall canvas partitions separated the back half of the shop. As Clint followed Jack around them, he saw a row of four doors built into one corner which contained the showers and bathrooms. Beside was a black metal frame supporting a round white plastic vessel as wide as his outstretched arms and twice as tall, that tapered at the bottom to a hose connection. Its smaller cousin sat to the right, and a plain electrical panel nestled between them. A grouping of steel barrels on wheeled bases were positioned beside it. A plastic shelving unit stacked with plain white cubes, like vintage refrigerators but connected with thick conduit, nestled in the corner. Tucked against the wall, from the shelving unit to the partition, was a tall van covered in a set of large tarps. Clint was only able to see the aggressive tread on the tires and the bottom of the matte-black wheels.

Jack stuck the tips of his fingers in his pockets and watched Clint try to take it all in. "Water filtration and rainwater harvestin', solar, wind power. You name it, we got it. The trucks and tractors seem to love the biodiesel, except when it gets really cold." Jack scratched his chin. "Heard way back in Germany there was a guy made it from dead cats. Christina'd kill me if I allowed that." He gave a shy smile. "But to be honest, outside of the old fryer oil, we ain't far off."

Clint scanned the operation a second time. "It's impressive."

Jack nodded. "Odell takes care of most of it. Junk runs, collects the oil for the bio, things like that."

"That probably explains the junkyard out back."

Jack nodded. "Sure enough does. It's amazin' what people will pay you to take off their hands, and what you can do with it. We keep what we can use, of course. We barter off what we can't." Jack checked his watch. "I know that wasn't much, but I'm thinkin' we should cut this short. Need to get on with chores and such."

"I need to grab a couple things from the truck." Clint motioned to the showers. "And I'd like to get washed up if you can spare the time."

Jack nodded. "Well, guess I won't say no to another cup of coffee. I'll see you at the house when you're done."

"Thank you. I won't be long."

Jack followed Clint out of the shop, turned all but one light off, then shuffled off in the direction of the house.

Clint waited for Jack to gain some distance, then walked around the front of the shop and to the side where his truck was parked. He swept the dusting of snow from the handle and the driver's side window, unlocked the door, and opened it. He listened for nearby footsteps, before reaching up under the dash to retrieve the cell phone he stashed before starting his journey. He flipped the screen open to confirm the battery level, then folded it and tucked it in his pants pocket. From there he closed and locked the door and side-stepped to dig around in the box closest to the cab. Lifting and shifting boxes and totes, he eventually dug out a crumpled duffle bag from the clutter. Alone or not, he chose not to check the contents then and there.

Standing at the front of the truck, he was meant to turn left, but instead what captured his attention was the footpath worn in the ground leading through a narrow break in the dense cluster of trees behind the shop. More than that was the speckled light in the open space beyond. Ignoring the twitch behind his eyes, the one telling him he wasn't safe in the dark, he lifted the strap of the duffle bag over his head and shoulder, then waded through the untouched snow, toward the path.

Once through the break in the trees, the world opened as he expected, but what it held was not.

Clint traced the path as it splintered out over soft, rolling hills, to patches of barren trees scattered around the border of the handful of acres contained by drooping barbed-wire fence. In among the patches of trees were a pop-top van, tow-behind camping trailers, and even a small motorhome. A few had solar panels reflecting in the muted light of a sun just starting its climb into the sky, or miniature turbine blades creaking in the breeze. Some had slight trails of smoke drifting up to blend with the monotone sky. Most showed signs of foot traffic to and from, but two of the tow-behinds were packed in with untouched snow. Halfway down, nearly blending into the edge of the treeline, was a double outhouse built from rough-hewn boards, the paint long since peeled away, but with some sort of insulation poking out between.

From a camper on the right, a woman in a long skirt walked out from the trees but stopped when she noticed Clint. She adjusted the blanket wrapped over her shoulders, raised a hand in greeting. Clint raised one back, then replaced it in his pocket. He resisted the urge to turn away. The woman searched for familiarity, but finding none, checked behind her, then hurried out of sight.

Clint lifted his hat to run a hand through greasy hair, overwhelmed by a feeling of being exposed. He tightened his hat down, then spun to head back to the shop to wash away what he could from the last couple days.

## NINE

Inside the house, showered and in a fresh change of clothes, Clint sat in the same chair he had earlier that morning with a straight back. His hands twisted his hat while his still damp hair hung in his eyes.

Christina sat in her usual spot with her hands around a coffee cup. Jack stood behind his chair. He set his cup down after draining it. "I expected the group to mind their manners a bit more'n they did. Sorry if that felt like you'd been thrown into the fire there."

Clint lowered his eyes. "It wasn't all that bad."

Jack frowned and rocked his head back and forth. "Odell needed to show off for whatever reason. Porter could'a been a little, I don't know, warmer."

"Don't really blame him. Given what's going on in the world, maybe it's good to be wary of strangers."

"Could be. Lots goin' on to want to keep yer distance from." Jack focused out the kitchen window. "But then, nothin's like it used to be." He raised a pointed finger. "The ranch, for instance. It ain't never been easy, this life, but at least in times past we had our own government's laws on our side." Jack patted the table with a flat hand. "But we've got a good group here. We all need a place to fit in. Have some direction. Feel safe. Anyhow, we do what we can. We find ways to make it work."

"Speaking of which,"—Christina stood, kissed her father on the cheek, then turned to go upstairs—"I need to head out."

Jack looked over at her. "You work today?"

"Jeannie's got some kind of appointment in Edmonton, so I picked up her shift."

"All right then. See you when you're home."

Christina nodded and climbed the creaky staircase.

Jack checked his watch. "Well, guess that means we should get to it."

"Yeah." Clint straightened the brim of his hat and set it on his head.

Jack narrowed one eye. "You said you're good at fixin' things?"

"Depends on what it is, but I tend to be able to figure it out."

Jack pulled at his ear. "Trucks been a bit rough lately, got some bad injectors in the mix from what I been told. Got all the parts to fix it up, but there's been more important things to worry 'bout. Think you'd be up to givin' it a go?"

Clint nodded. "Haven't messed with a twelve-valve in a while, but I'm sure it'll come back to me."

A slow smile came to Jack's face. "All right then. I'll get you set up after we check the herd. Let's get to it."

———

Clint adjusted his position, perched over the front fender of Jack's truck, and planted one foot on top of the tire with the other stretched out into the air. He torqued one last bolt near the back of the engine, then hopped down into a flurry of dirty shop towels and sent one of the many cans of empty brake fluid toward the garage door. A sneaker-clad foot tilted up to stop it before it escaped outside.

The boy stood with one hand on the strap of the backpack over his shoulder and tucked a length of hair, dark but not black, behind his ear with the other. Except, Clint wondered if boy was the right way to put it. He set the wrench on top of the fender, then took the cleanest rag within reach to wipe his hands down, more to give them something to do than anything else. "Hey."

"You're new."

"I am."

The boy watched him.

Clint searched amber eyes, the same as his mother. "You're Christina's son."

The boy nodded.

Clint finished digging between his fingers with the rag, stepped forward, and extended his hand. "Clint."

The boy paused, then extended his own. "Kieran."

"Good to meet you."

Kieran nodded.

"Grandpa know you're working on his truck?"

Clint turned back to the task at hand. "Wouldn't be under the hood if he didn't."

"He usually has me give him a hand."

"Oh." Clint averted his eyes. "He said it was past due on some things, asked me to have a go. My initiation, I suppose."

Kieran looked down and tapped the empty brake cleaner can over to a corner. "Yeah, things have been busy, I guess."

"School?"

"Yeah. Mostly."

"Mostly." Clint balled up the rag in his hand and tossed it toward a pile of others on the floor. "I didn't ever go to university or anything like that, but I get the feeling I know what mostly means."

It was Kieran's turn to avert his eyes.

"You and your grandad are pretty close?"

"Yeah, he's always been there for me. For Mom too."

"You're lucky to have that. Not everyone does. Or they don't see it when they do."

Kieran shrugged. "Yeah."

Clint noticed a hint of sorrow in the boy's eyes. "Sorry, I didn't mean to…"

Kieran shook his head. "It's okay. There's a reason we don't talk about Dad much."

Clint scratched at his jaw. "Sorry."

Kieran looked over his shoulder. "I should head in."

"Sure. I'm assuming I'll be seeing you in a bit."

Kieran nodded, then turned and walked to the house.

Clint rested a hand on the truck's fender. He stared at the cluttered floor, but it was fleeting images of his kids that he saw. The distance, both physical and emotional, bored into his heart. He wanted to pull the phone from his pocket and call them, but he let it be. Instead, he kicked at the garbage, pushing it into a pile so he could finish the task at hand, and get things cleaned up.

## TEN

Brandon tied a white apron around his waist as he rounded the corner to the prep area. Tiff hunched over a green cutting board that sat crooked on top of a stainless worktable, peeling russets bigger than her fist. She looked up but immediately focused back on her task. "Hey, Brandon."

Brandon looked Tiff up and down, her wrinkled and stained chef jacket and apron, her caramel brown hair tucked back but loose at her temples, and the beaded perspiration on her forehead and upper lip. "You all right, Tiff?"

Tiff wiped her forehead with her arm then grabbed another potato. "Not really, running a bit behind."

Brandon pulled a hair net from the box mounted to the wall next to him and slipped it over his head and the tops of his ears. He grabbed the spare peeler from beside the open sack of potatoes and joined in. "Been a long day?"

"Christ, you don't know the half of it." Tiff dropped a peeled potato into the bucket of water on the floor beside her, then grabbed another. "I've been at this almost twelve hours already."

Brandon finished peeling his first potato and dropped it in the bucket. "Why didn't you call me earlier?"

Tiff cleared the phlegm from her throat. "Too busy."

"Where's Cesar at?"

"Off today. Doctor's appointment or something." Tiff dropped another potato in the bucket. As it was close enough to full, she bent down to grab the handle then shuffled off to the walk-in cooler with it.

Brandon followed. "Are you up for a break soon?"

Tiff set the bucket down at an angle, nearly dumping the whole thing across the tile floor. "Just got back from a few days off. Won't be able to get away again for a while." Tiff pulled a sheet pan of seasoned chicken legs from the rack beside the walk-in door.

Brandon shifted to one side to let Tiff pass, but she stopped and held the tray out to him.

"Here, stick it in for me."

Brandon smirked. "That's what she said."

Tiff didn't flirt in a harmless way as Brandon expected. She didn't respond at all. Instead, she pulled out a second tray, then kicked the walk-in door closed behind her as she walked the tray over to a double-stack oven and slid the tray inside. She moved down the cook line, leaving the oven doors open.

Brandon watched her the whole time, a frown pulling at his lips, then as she stopped in front of a large stock pot sitting tall on the range, he stepped forward to put his tray into the oven.

Tiff recoiled and swallowed hard to contain a hitch in her throat, but it was not enough. She coughed, open-mouthed, over the pot of gravy, her arm halfway to her face at best.

Brandon closed the oven doors and turned to Tiff. "What was that?"

Tiff's face was pale, her arm still bent in front of her. "Nothin'." She grabbed the tall whisk sticking out of the pot and stirred the contents.

Brandon stood a few steps away and crossed his arms. "Where'd you go on your days off?"

Tiff grimaced as she finished stirring the pot of simmering gravy. She tapped the whisk on the top of the pot, then let it sit again at the side. "Had to go check in on my mom. She ain't been well lately."

"That's not good. She still in Portage la Prairie?"

"I've been trying to get her to move out here, but she doesn't want to sell the house." Tiff reached down to turn off the burner under the stock pot. "Anyway, I still need another bucket of potatoes. Come give me a hand."

## ELEVEN

Clint pulled a pair of canvas work gloves from his back pocket as he passed the front of the shop and walked to the pile of long logs stacked near the treeline separating the yard from the open space and campers beyond.

Porter worked beside the logs and an empty trailer hooked up to a four-wheeled ATV. He swung a big splitting axe into a wide stump, shattering the calm afternoon air again and again, until all that remained was a scattered pile of usable pieces. He wore nothing more than heavy boots, worn cargo pants, and a sleeveless undershirt. Warm vapor rose from his crown and shoulders like his skin was barely able to contain a simmering fire underneath.

Clint raised a hand as he stopped well back from the radius of chopped wood. Porter looked up but offered no formal acknowledgment.

Clint cleared the warble from his throat, tried not to focus on Porter's bloodshot eye. "Hey. Jack figured you could use a hand. So…here I am."

Porter pointed with the splitter in his hand to a weathered

stump with a smaller axe sticking up from the top a few paces away. Clint nodded, then took his position. After breaking down the first couple stumps, he spoke up out of a sense of awkwardness.

"So, you from around here?"

"Yup." Porter brought the axe down.

Clint set up a new stump. "How long've you been set up here with Jack?"

When Porter brought the axe down again, it rang out like a gunshot. "Few years now."

"Seems like—"

Porter raised his free hand. "Listen, we don't need to do this."

"Sorry." Clint held his axe at the ready but stared at his feet. "Just nervous, which is kinda new for me. Didn't have much of a problem dealing with people before…"

Thin lipped, Porter nodded. He finished splitting his last piece then set the axe into the ragged old stump he was using to back up his work. "It changed a lot of things. I'll give you that." He reset one of his ear buds, then bent to collect split pieces and toss them into the trailer.

"How…" Clint second guessed his grip before he brought his axe down. "How did you fair out here?"

Porter paused and looked to Clint.

"I mean, you know, away from the city and all."

Porter finished clearing the wood from the ground around him, then turned back to his axe. "Could have been worse. Could have been better."

"Sounds about right." Clint unzipped his jacket and shrugged it off. He set up a new stump and swung.

From there, he did his best to keep pace with Porter until the pile of cut logs had been cleared. The trailer nearly overflowed with split wood, and a pile just as big sat next to it.

Porter set the splitter into the big stump, then stepped over to Clint and held out his hand. "Thank you. It's rare that anyone is able to keep up with me."

Clint took the big man's hand, like a bag of hot stones, and tried not to wince as he shook it. "Not sure if I'd call that keeping up, but I appreciate it."

Footsteps in the snow, echoing on the other side of the trees, took Porter's attention. He side-stepped to allow a clearer view of the path toward the trailers.

Clint recognized the woman from their awkward encounter that morning. The heavy jacket she wore over her plain, ankle-length dress looked like it belonged to Porter. Or it used to, at least. Long black braids hung over her shoulders. The only jewelry Clint could see was the gold band on her left ring finger. She held a tight smile, keeping her soft, brown eyes focused on Porter as she walked up to face him, shoulder to opposite shoulder. She reached up on the tiptoes of her insulated boots for a single kiss.

Porter put a hand on her waist. "Dinner time already?"

"Not quite. I told Andie I would help with getting things ready, though."

"Good thing I've worked up an appetite."

The woman turned to stand beside Porter.

When Clint looked up, Porter pulled the woman closer. The big man's smile was gone, and his jaw tight. Clint lifted his hat and scratched at his head while he checked over his shoulder, then reluctantly turned back to the couple.

Porter broke the silence. "Clint, this is May. My wife."

"Oh." Clint held up a hand. "Nice to, uh, meet you. Official like."

May nodded, eyes darting to Clint and away, then back. "You too." She looked up to Porter. "I should get to the house."

Porter nodded. "I will see you soon."

May reached up for another kiss. "Neghanighita."

"Neghanighita."

May turned away from Clint and cut fresh tracks in the snow around the shop until she was out of sight.

Porter searched the sky for the position of the sun. "Take the trailer out front, stack everything in the shed beside the old barn. I'll start hauling the rest out back. When you're done, you can help me finish up."

"Sure, yeah." Clint picked up his jacket and put it on, then straddled the ATV and hit the ignition. As he pulled away, Porter stacked cut wood in the crook of his arm and lumbered off toward the trailers.

# TWELVE

Clint followed Porter through the front door but stopped in the porch after slipping his boots off. He leaned against the door frame with his fingers tucked in his pockets and watched as Porter raised a hand to May on his way to wash up. May smiled as she finished clearing vegetable scraps from the counter, her eyes never leaving him. When Porter returned and took his seat at the table, Clint pushed forward and went to wash up himself.

He was last to sit, outside of Andie and Christina who joined after they had finished placing the night's meal on the table. Clint was about to reach out but noticed the silence, tucked chins, and closed eyes in time. Clint lowered his own chin in solidarity, or guilt perhaps, but his eyes stayed open.

Jack held Christina's hand with a slight tremor. Christina held Kieran's hand as solid as a heavy root in the ground.

"Lord, we thank you for this day, for our health, and for this bounty before us. We ask you to continue to watch over us, and to keep the ones we love safe." Jack's chin developed a tremble, then he punctuated saying grace with a sharp nod. "Amen."

When the table echoed Jack's sentiment, he smiled and opened his damp eyes. "All right then. Dig in, everyone."

Hands unclasped then reached for the dishes and bowls scattered in front of them. Clint kept his eyes on Jack just a moment longer, unable to turn away as he fought the hitch in his throat. He only diverted as Patch passed along a bowl of boiled carrots. By the time conversation faded, replaced with the clinking of cutlery on plates, Clint had a healthy stack of sliced chicken, peas, carrots, and a mound of slightly lumpy mashed potatoes smothered with gravy in front of him. As he ate, the warmth in his belly radiated out, easing his strained muscles and weary mind. He sank into his chair and eavesdropped as chatter among the group started up again.

Jack ripped open a bun and took a bite. He waved what was left in Kieran's direction. "How was school for you today?"

Kieran shrugged and pushed a path through the mashed potatoes on his plate with his fork. "It was okay."

Jack waited for more, but it didn't come. "That all we get?"

Kieran sat up straighter and pursed his lips. "It was math and English and gym. There's not much going on with winter break coming. Not sure what else to say."

Jack nodded. "That's all I was lookin' for, Grandson. Just want to make sure everythin's goin' as well as it can."

Kieran nodded and took the first bite of his food.

Jack changed the direction of the lean in his chair. "You able to get the woodsheds topped up?"

Porter held the back of his hand to his mouth while he chewed and nodded. "It's done. With a little help, of course."

Jack's eyes shifted to Clint, then back to Porter, a sly smile pulling on his lips. "Good to see everyone's settlin' in. One more thing to be grateful for."

Clint nodded, unsure what to say in response.

Jack loaded up a forkful of food. "Guess we should look at getting you set up out back tomorrow or the day after."

Clint swallowed, then picked at his teeth with his tongue while he worked Jack's comment out. "You mean the campers?"

"That I do. We have a couple available at the moment, if memory serves."

Odell didn't look up as he scraped what food remained on his plate into a nondescript pile. "It's on the list to get cleaned out first thing tomorrow mornin'."

"There we are then. Tomorrow or the day after it is."

Odell chewed and swallowed. "May want to wait until Sunday, heard we've got some weather comin' in."

"Well, normally Sunday's 're for rest, more out of habit than for any religious inclination, but sounds like it won't take much to get you settled."

Clint locked eyes with Jack, though he had to focus to maintain it. "I appreciate it. I really do." He lowered his head to his plate. "I been meaning to ask about all that. I mean, not with any expectation for myself. Just wanted to understand the situation."

"Guess we forgot to touch upon that, but I assure it was more for our own peace of mind than anything else." Jack leaned forward, resting his elbows on the edge of the table. "I'm sure you got most of it figured out, but everyone here has their own spot in the back forty. We generally keep one or two set aside for summer help or out-of-town family, on the rare occasion that happens."

Andie lifted her eyes from her plate but kept her head low. "We have to be selective, for what I hope are obvious reasons."

Jack nodded. "Don't need too many noses in our business is all." He chewed on his lip in a way that suggested to Clint that he wanted to say more, wanted to open the door a little wider, but he didn't.

For the rest of the meal, outside of the odd whispered comment or request to pass a dish for seconds, little was said. All but Christina and Andie went on their way once dinner was finished. Jack retired to the living room to catch the end of the six o'clock news. Kieran joined him but focused on his phone instead of the television. Clint stayed to help with the dishes, but an uneasiness weighed on him after Jack's comments, and it wouldn't let go. So, with the damp dish towels hung, the lights dimmed, and the chairs tucked under the table, he excused himself for the night.

# THIRTEEN

Clint followed the red-stained valley toward the darkening western sky. Streetlights flickered, but never fully lit. Houses lining the street remained indistinct, blending into each other to the point of being little more than background noise.

His footing faltered every few steps, not only due to the uneven ground, but because of an unnatural pull of gravity, like his boots were caked with mud and rocks instead of blood-stained snow. He trudged on, the weight in his body accompanied by something much heavier that settled over his mind. Sadness with no direction, without a name, or perhaps with too many.

He wiped at his eye with the back of his hand, then glanced the way he had come. Deep in the distance, the sidewalk filled with movement. A dark mass, surging forward at unnatural speed, but without sound. As details came into focus, Clint saw flailing limbs, blood-soaked clothing and skin, exposed bones. He also saw eyes filled with rage, and reflections of the setting sun.

Clint did not hesitate. He turned, released the carton of

milk, and ran. Or at least he tried to. He scrambled and clawed his way forward, as if attempting to sprint across the deep end of a swimming pool. Panic built behind his eyes and clouded his vision, turning the slit of light on the horizon to haze. He did not dare look back. He kept pushing forward, trying not to lose his footing.

Seconds later, sooner than it should have, his futile attempt at escape came to an end. The mass of bodies reared up around him like the gaping maw of an elder god. As the shadow took what dim light surrounded Clint, so too did it take what fight remained in him. He stumbled to his knees and brought his hands over his head in time for the wave of broken bodies to crush him.

FOURTEEN

Jack stepped out onto the porch as Clint shuffled across the yard and neared the house, hunched over with his hands stuffed into the pouch of his sweater, and the hood lowered over his puffy eyes. The stubble on his chin did not help his disheveled appearance. Jack scowled as Clint stopped at the bottom of the porch steps. "Hell, son, you look like shit."

Clint shrugged but did not make eye contact. "Feel it too."

Jack pushed up on his hat. "Sorry, that ain't the greetin' I'm sure you were lookin' for. Good mornin', Clint."

Clint cleared his throat. "Mornin'."

"Anything I can do for you?"

"No fault of the facilities, or your hospitality. Just can't seem to get much in the way of sleep."

"Well, get yourself a coffee and meet me back out here once you're set. After we check on the cattle, I'm heading out with Duncan and Odell for a little road trip. I was hoping you could spend the afternoon with Patch out in the shop. He's got a few things he was hoping to get a hand with."

Clint nodded, then stepped around Jack and toward the front door.

"Might want to grab a better jacket and some proper gloves while you're at it."

"Yes, sir." Clint stepped inside and eased the door closed behind him.

———

As the sun moved low on the horizon, Jack hobbled up the porch steps with a case of fresh pork sausages under one arm, and an oversized reusable fabric tote filled with loaves of bread looped around his other hand. He opened the front door, then stood aside. Duncan shuffled through, cradling a smoked ham in each arm. Deep in the kitchen, Andie cleared space on the counter for the new arrivals.

"Those look amazing. Pine Meadows colony?"

Duncan nodded. "Came out of the smoker this morning."

"Good timing, then."

Jack set the case of sausages down and flopped the bag of bread on top. "Still got a box of perogies in the back of the truck, too."

Duncan nodded. "I'll get 'em."

Jack patted Duncan's shoulder on the way by. "Thank you." He rested back on the counter, only leaning forward for a kiss on the cheek as Christina entered the room.

"You're back."

"That we are. Well, Duncan and I. Odell won't be far behind, he had a couple things to finish up yet."

"Long day."

"Yes, ma'am. Just a bit."

"Should I set him a plate?"

"Pardon?"

"Odell. Should I set him a plate?"

"How much time we got?"

Christina scanned the kitchen. "Half hour, maybe a bit more."

"Probably best if you do."

"Okay, then."

Jack scratched at his chin. "Anyone seen Clint lately?"

"Out in the shop, last I saw." Andie cut open the case of sausages to portion and freeze. "But it's sure been quiet for a bit."

Jack crossed his arms, and his face pinched, but he did not say anything.

Christina wiped her hands on a dish towel before setting it on the counter. "Andie, you okay here for a few minutes?"

"Shouldn't be a problem."

"I'll be right back." Christina gave her father another peck on the cheek, then rushed out the front door.

FIFTEEN

Clint drew his hands over his head, fingertips pulling down on his eyelids, forcing him to witness his fate. Instead of consuming him, though, the horde split, rushing past him like an avalanche around a rocky crag. They pushed and jostled, only grazing him as they went. With the silent deluge flowing around him, Clint raised his head to the sun as the last of its light faded. It was then he sensed a change in the rushing bodies, a change in the space between him and them. A hand rested on his shoulder, and someone spoke his name.

Clint spun around. The figure protecting him from the horde hunched their shoulders forward as they lowered their arm. Dark, matted hair hung over their face. Clint's breath caught in his throat as a scream threatened to let loose.

The figure lifted their head, and their hair fell away. Pale, freckled skin surrounded pained cobalt eyes.

Krystal.

Her thin lips turned down, mouthed a single word.

Why?

When her lips parted again, a cascade of black tar trailed

down her chin and splattered on the ground. Her eyebrows pinched. Without a sound, she asked again.

Why?

Clint bared his teeth and his jaw clenched tight. He pressed his hands over his ears.

Krystal's head tilted and her chin trembled, pulling her seeping mouth into a frown.

*Why?*

Clint strained to look away, but the strength eluded him. Krystal stepped forward, reaching out with both hands, scarred and bleeding, nails torn from their beds. Crimson tears seeped from her eyes as she clenched her fists. She bared stained teeth and bellowed into Clint's soul. One word...

# SIXTEEN

Clint jolted awake, eyes wide, body tense.

"You okay there?"

Clint looked all around, focusing on what could have been a figure hiding in the shadows of the far corner of the shop. He blinked until his eyes adjusted, and the figure disappeared. "Think so."

"Are you sure?"

Clint landed his gaze on Christina, then ran his hands down his face. "No."

Christina shifted her stance and crossed her arms. "So, who is Krystal?"

Clint looked at the shadows, searching for a face. "What?"

"Krystal. You called her name. She your wife?"

Clint sat forward, leaned on his knees, and cleared his throat. "Cousin."

A worried smile "Not like a kissin' cousin situation, is it?"

Clint straightened and scowled. "What? No."

"Sorry. It's just, the way you called out. It sounded serious."

Clint shook his head. Any words he could offer caught in his throat.

Christina studied Clint's face, and her expression softened. "You lost her."

"Lost a lot of people."

"She was important, though."

"She was."

Christina pulled over a rolling stool and sat, wrapped her hands over her knees. "Can you tell me about her?"

"Maybe. One day."

Christina hesitated, then fanned her hands out. "Today is one day."

Clint looked away, not to the corners of the shop, not to the shadows. "Yeah, suppose it is."

"Listen, if you're not ready to talk, then don't. It's just—"

"No. It's fine." Clint rubbed at his temple, though it did little to clear his mind. "If you want to know, I guess you should know."

# SEVENTEEN

The sun had nearly set on Clint's second day at the hunting camp. He found no sign of either Krystal or their customers beyond days-old tracks, even though he had spent most of his waking hours tracing the usual trails and as far beyond as he could manage on his own.

With the fire burned down to little more than coals, and a half-full plate of beans on the ground beside him, Clint stared up to the evening sky. He let the constant loop of what-ifs continue their rampage through his mind in the hope that maybe this time a puzzle piece would fall into place, that something resembling an answer might be found.

He blinked hard before rubbing at his eyes. The thought rose in his mind to pack up, head out early the next morning, and come back with more help. It was only after his attention was drawn by movement in the trees that he noticed a column of black smoke wafting into the northern sky a few kilometers away. He barely had time to stand before someone stumbled into the camp.

Clint reached for the barrel of the rifle propped against his chair, but instead of raising it, he hung it from the crook of his arm. Ready, but not. He knew that out of anyone, it was Krystal who would survive, that she would be the one to beat the odds.

Relief twitched across his face as the fire light reached far enough to confirm it was her. That relief faded as she neared, though. One leg dragged along, the toe of her boot never leaving the ground. Blood trailed from a cut over her knee, and from another gash on her shoulder. Vacant eyes stared out from sandy-brown hair, matted over her forehead with sweat. Each hand grasped a crimson-edged blade.

Clint knew the look all too well. He dropped the rifle and ran to take his cousin's arm a moment before she released the blades and collapsed. Clint scanned her up and down. "Jesus —what the fuck happened to you?"

Krystal groaned. Her lips parted like she wanted to speak, but nothing came.

Clint eased her toward the fire, sat her down, then ran to a small fabric cooler under the table at the outdoor kitchen for a bottle of water. On the way back he twisted the cap off and held it out for her.

Krystal raised a hand to cup the bottle and tilted it back. After swallowing twice, she lowered it, not wiping at the trail of moisture on her chin.

Clint knelt in front of her, scanning her face and body. "Krys, what the fuck happened?"

Krystal shook her head slowly and stared into the trees, not blinking.

Clint set a hand on her knee. She flinched and smacked it away. Her wide eyes turned on him.

"Krystal. Come on."

Krystal's gaze fell. "I want to go."

"We should get you cleaned up at least."

"I'm fine."

"No, you fuckin' aren't."

"I want to go."

"What about the guys—"

"Clint."

"What happened to—"

"*Clint.*"

Clint froze as his name echoed through the trees.

"I want to go home. *Now.*"

Not another word was spoken. Clint packed the essentials and doused the fire. He led on their way out, the harsh beam of a flashlight sweeping the path ahead. Krystal trailed behind in the dark, loosely following his footprints in the snow.

Clint kept the windows down on the ride home to help combat the smell. The wafting breeze and drone of the car's tires took the place of the radio. The consistency of it made the hours-long journey seem shorter. It was the only thing that did.

Krystal spent the ride curled up against the passenger-side door, drifting in and out of a fitful sleep. More than once, she snapped awake, arms shooting up to shield herself. Eventually, her breathing would slow, and her eyes would close again.

The sun showed on the horizon as Clint parked the car in front of Krystal's house. He turned the ignition off, then held his hand against his mouth while he stifled a yawn. "You need a hand up?"

Krystal shook her head.

"I can stay. I mean, I need to bring the car back anyway. We've got a lot to figure out."

She stared out the window to her front door.

"We're going to talk about this later. Right?"

She hesitated but nodded.

"Good. Okay."

Krystal reached up and fumbled to open the door. She angled out and paused. "Clint, I—"

"Hey, Krys, it's okay. Whatever happened, we'll sort it out." Clint pulled the keys from the ignition, threaded off the car key and handed the rest to Krystal. "Here. You might need these."

Krystal took the keys and nodded without turning toward Clint. She pushed herself up, closed the car door, then limped up the walkway. After opening the front door of her house, she glanced back. Clint raised a hand. Krystal raised a hand in return. He started the car and pulled away from the curb, watching his cousin in the rearview as he drove on.

# EIGHTEEN

"I expected to be back after a few hours of sleep. Start working things out. I didn't really know anything. What happened. Where everyone got off to. I just knew it wasn't good." Clint picked at calloused skin on his hands. "I learned after, from the investigators on the case, that when Krystal got home, she washed her face, changed her clothes, took a handful of change from the mason jar she kept on the kitchen counter, and walked out the front door. They couldn't piece together where she was for thirty-two minutes between passing the liquor store on Ross Street and walking up to the grocery store three blocks away, but the rest was easy enough to figure out.

"She went through the front door at 8:48 a.m. and made her first pass around the perimeter of the store. She grabbed a loaf of bread, and a one liter carton of milk that she rubbed across her forehead before tuckin' it under one arm. On the second lap, she slowed down some. Stopped once or twice to stare at a display, would pick somethin' up for a better look, but in the end, put it down and move on. On her third trip around, she diverted to the pharmacy. They said she was standin' in front of the pain medication when it happened. She dropped the bread and the milk before fallin' to her knees... I'm sure you can figure out the rest." Clint closed his eyes. "After she puked up that black shit, some poor kid stocking shelves, for whatever reason, came to help her out. She was upright just long enough to drop him."

Clint turned away as images from the store's security cameras played out silently behind his eyelids. Krystal clawing at the kid's face, biting at his hands as he tried to fend her off. When others, stupid enough to intervene, came to the kid's rescue, Krystal shifted her focus.

"It only lasted a few minutes, but she managed to hurt twelve people. That number doubled after she found her way out the front door.

"Not that anyone ever said so to my face, or confirmed in any way, but that was when things flared up again. Got worse because of a mutation or variant or whatever they ended up blaming it on. I'm sure you know the rest. The infected lived for months instead of days. Sometimes longer, I've heard. The vaccines stopped workin'. The government started building fences and walls instead of tryin' to figure out how to stop it." Clint looked up to Christina. "And here we are."

Christina opened her mouth to say something, but it took time for the words to come. "I'm so sorry. I...don't know what to say."

"Ain't nothin' to fuckin' say." Clint sighed and his shoulders slumped. "Sorry. I didn't mean..."

Christina held up a hand. "No. Don't worry. It's okay."

They sat in silence, not looking at each other, or anything else in particular. Eventually, Christina stood. She stuck the tips of her fingers in the back pockets of her jeans. She turned to the door, then back to Clint. She leaned as if she was about to step toward him, perhaps to console, to offer some sort of condolence, but instead she shifted her stance and walked away. "We're working on dinner. Come on in once you're ready."

After the small door closed, Clint held his hands over the stinging in his eyes.

# NINETEEN

With dinner eaten and the table clear, Clint eased his chair back and set his hands flat to push himself up. A deck of cards wrapped in a thin elastic band hit the table, along with a wooden cribbage board, and then a fresh bottle of Crown Royal whisky with a black label, and three short, crystal glasses. Jack pointed to Clint. "It ain't necessarily an order, but keep your backside on that chair. I may not be, but the night is still young."

Clint moved his hands to the arms of his chair and leaned back with a nod.

Jack cracked the seal on the whisky bottle and poured three healthy portions. "Can I interest you in a drink?"

Clint shook his head. "I'm good, thanks."

Jack capped the bottle. "Beer in the fridge if you prefer."

"No. Thank you."

Jack set the bottle on the table. "Coffee, then?"

Clint stifled a yawn. "That'll work."

Christina drifted past. "Just started a pot. I'll bring it over when it's ready."

"Remember what I said 'bout it not bein' an order." Jack eyed Clint. "If you need to rest, maybe you should call it."

Clint stared out the kitchen window, just catching the glow of the sodium light buzzing over the barn's big door. "I'm okay. Seems I had my chance to catch up earlier."

Jack laughed. "So, I heard. Guess I been meaning to ask, you two got the electrical system sorted out?"

"We got done what Patch wanted to get done, finished early, even. I guess that gave me a moment to rest my eyelids, but I promise it was work before play."

Jack's smile grew, and he nodded. "That's the way we like it. As long as the work gets done, ain't no reason to worry." He reached out for one of the short glasses and took a sip. He smacked his lips and exhaled as he measured what was left in the glass with his eyes. "But we never forget the play aspect. As much as is reasonable, at any rate." He sat in his usual seat, unwrapped the cards, then cracked the side of the deck on the table. "You play?"

Clint glanced at the crib board. "Not something I ever picked up."

"Maybe it's time to learn?"

Clint allowed a tired smile. "Maybe another day."

Jack nodded. "Porter, you in?"

Porter leaned his forearms against the edge of the table. "Maybe just one."

"Miss May, don't fret, I won't ask."

May smiled and leaned into Porter's shoulder.

"Duncan, you in?"

"Think I'll pass tonight." Duncan leaned forward and pulled one of the short glasses close to him. "This I'll partake in, though."

"Odell, what about you?"

Odell had leaned forward on one elbow. He mulled over the question a moment before answering. "You know what, I think I'm going to head out. It's been a day."

Jack nodded. "See you at breakfast, then."

"That you will." Odell raised a hand to the room, shuffled toward the front door, stepped into his boots, then walked out into the night.

With the players set, Andie and Patch out to the yard with the tray of scraps, and Kieran off doing teenaged things, Jack pulled the crib board closer and flipped it on its face. He slid open a flat piece of metal and picked out three sets of pegs. With the board right-side up, he set the pegs. Dealing the cards, he ended with five in front of Porter, five in front of Christina's chair, and five in front of himself. He set a single card face down next to the rest of the deck.

While Jack finished the setup, Clint raised his head to the radio on top of the fridge as Johnny Cash sang out from the tinny speakers. "How do you fit a transmission in a lunchbox?"

Jack gave a toothy grin. "Well, much like in life, the answers are there if you pay attention."

Christina came to the table soon after. She set three of the coffee mugs looped through her fingers down near the crib board and took the last to set down in front of Clint, then poured it to the brim.

"Thank you."

Christina looked into Clint's eyes and smiled, then took her seat.

Clint sipped, winced at the heat, then wrapped his hands around the mug and focused on the game. Each player pulled a single card from their hand and set it beside the deck. Jack motioned to Porter, who split the deck and left the eight of spades facing up.

Jack sorted his cards, then set his hand face down on the table. "Ladies first."

Christina exhaled with her free hand over the fanned cards. "Not a lot of good options. Eight?"

Porter stared at his cards. "You can say that again. Eleven."

"I'll agree that I could've done better." Jack pinched the top of one card, then the card next to it. "Eighteen, I suppose."

Christina allowed a small smile. "Twenty-five for two." She laid the card, advanced her peg, then pulled the remaining glass of whisky toward her.

Porter tossed a six down. "And that makes thirty-one."

"Nicely done." Jack laid a nine down, then reached for his drink. "Hopefully that doesn't get me in too much trouble."

Christina set down a king. "Hopefully that answers your question."

Porter frowned and dropped a card on his pile. "Twenty-nine. Just to confirm."

Jack laughed. "I'll have to pass on that." He raised his glass and drained it. When he set it down, he smiled wide with flushed cheeks. "This may be a long night."

TWENTY

Brandon lay in bed, his head propped up against the wall and one hand rubbing at his temple. The overhead light was out, the screen on his e-reader as dim as it could go without being off. He reached with his thumb to turn the page but closed his eyes while it advanced.

The derrickhand in the next room was on a phone call home. The thin walls, seemingly for show more than anything else, did little to contain the agitation in their voice. Brandon tried hard to focus on his reading, but the raised voice, combined with the migraine creeping in around the wrinkles and folds of his brain prevented that from happening. As the conversation wavered and escalated, Brandon raised a hand to hammer on the wall. Before it made contact, he stared at his shaking fist as if he did not recognize it. Because, in some way, it was foreign to him. With everything that had happened over the previous eighteen months he thought all of his anger and frustration had been used up. Or that he buried what was left. Not deep enough, apparently. He brushed away the moment of worry, swiping it aside like a page of his book. Out of sight, but perhaps not out of mind.

Somewhere down the hall, two voices called out in anger, whether at each other or someone else was uncertain. A door slammed, then an uneasy silence returned. Brandon guided the fingers at his temple across his forehead. Things sometimes got tense around the full moon, but he could have sworn one just passed. What caused the current mood, he did not want to consider, but he was as successful at diverting his attention from that train of thought as he was at focusing on his book.

He lowered his e-reader to his lap. The air stifled his breath. Too thick. Too warm. Warmer than it should have been for how cold it was outside. He flipped his e-reader closed, slunk off his bed, then eased himself to standing. He checked the lock on his door, drew the sliding window as far open as it would go, then rolled into bed on his side. Reaching blind, he pulled a single thin sheet over his head as heavy boots hammered along the hall outside his room.

# TWENTY-ONE

Clint nursed his coffee and watched the trio play. As the third round neared its end, he thought he had a decent grasp on things, both in the card play and family dynamics, but he was tired enough that he was not entirely sure. Christina won the first hand. Jack took his pegs home to confirm his second win. Duncan groaned along with Christina and Porter, as he had the entire time.

Jack collected his cards and flipped them face down on top of the deck. "Well, I think that about does it for me." He picked up his glass, but as barely a drop clung to the bottom, put it down and pushed it toward the near empty bottle of whisky. He smiled with warmth beyond the effects of the alcohol. "Have a good night. See you all in the morning."

May grabbed Porter's arm and locked eyes.

Porter nodded. "Time for us to turn in as well."

Jack took his glass to set it in the sink on his way upstairs.

May pulled on her jacket, and after a quick goodbye, headed out the front door ahead of Porter.

Christina collected the cards, shuffled, broke the deck in two, then shuffled again before setting them down. She also reset the pegs on the board.

Duncan spun his quarter-full glass with uncoordinated fingers. Every couple of turns he glanced over to Christina, much like he had been doing all night.

Christina leaned in her chair and focused on Clint. "How about you, time for bed?"

Clint looked to the clock on the wall, then the cold cup of coffee in front of him. "Not sure. Might've caught my third wind."

"Well,"—Christina unscrewed the cap from the whisky and topped up her glass—"maybe if you don't have anything better to do you should come down here and keep me company until it is."

Duncan straightened in his chair.

Clint looked from Duncan, to Christina, and back, though neither of them noticed. "Uh, okay." He stood, paused a moment, deciding which way to go, then walked to the opposite end of the table. He looked at the available chairs, hand wavering over the back of May's, then Porter's, before pulling it out and sitting down. The warmth as he sat made him uncomfortable for more than one reason, but it might have been better than sitting shoulder to shoulder with Duncan.

Christina sipped at her glass, then picked up the deck of cards and started dealing. Six to Clint, six to herself, with the remainder of the deck set down between them.

"What's this."

Christina fanned her cards and sorted them. "You've watched long enough. Time to jump in."

Duncan focused on the table, perhaps at the empty space where his hand should have landed. He lifted his glass to drain it, then pushed himself back. He walked out the front door without a word. A gust of cold air swirled around the room, bringing with it a few errant snowflakes, before the door closed.

Clint watched Duncan, long after he had gone. "What was that?"

"Oh, you know." Christina pulled two cards from her hand and set them down next to the deck. "I have to be careful not to give him hope of being anything more than friends. If that's even the right way to put it. Unfortunately, it comes across as being a bit cold sometimes."

"He's got a thing for you." It was a statement. "I wondered."

"We're in a bit of a closed ecosystem, doesn't have any other options. At least, that's what I tell myself. Lucky for me, he's harmless."

Clint nodded, even though he was not sure he agreed. He picked up the cards in front of him. "What do I do here?"

"Take two and put them in the crib." Christina pointed to the cards she had just discarded.

Clint picked two of his own at random and added them on top.

Christina rapped her knuckles on the deck. "Cut it."

Clint reached out to split the deck, then turned it over. The Jack of clubs faced up.

Christina smiled. "Thank you."

"You're welcome?"

"You start."

"Six." He dropped the six of diamonds.

Christina smiled with a certain glint in her eye but stayed on the game. "Eight."

Clint followed up immediately. "Ten. For two?"

"Good." Christina waited for Clint to move his peg, then flipped another two onto the table. "Twelve for six."

"Shit."

"Don't worry, the game's not over yet."

Clint laid down a seven. "Nineteen."

"Twenty-two."

"Twenty-eight."

"Thirty."

Clint sighed again and collected his cards.

Christina arranged hers in front of her. "Fifteen two, four, six, and six is twelve." She reached out to advance her peg then looked over at Clint's cards. "You sure you don't know what you're doing here?"

Clint shrugged. "Maybe I'm a quick learner."

"Oh, I don't doubt it."

Clint focused on his cards. "Fifteen for two, four, and a pair should be six. I think."

"Yup, you're good." Christina picked up the crib. "Three jacks for six. Not bad." She collected the cards after moving her peg and dropped the deck in front of Clint.

Clint picked it up. "You guys do this every Saturday night?"

"Mostly. Started when I was a kid."

"Did your dad teach you?"

Christina shook her head as she gulped down a swig of whisky. "Mom taught me. Back then Dad was usually too busy."

Clint cleared his throat. "Your mom, I've sort of been meanin' to ask, but I wasn't sure how…"

"I think you've earned the right to ask pretty much whatever you want at this point. Pretty much." Christina searched the uncomfortable expression on Clint's face. "She's in Lethbridge. Living her best life, whatever that means."

"Oh, I thought…"

Christina smiled without joy. "You're thinking of Iris. Dad's second wife."

"Guess I am."

"Never seen him pine like I have for her. Don't get me wrong, she was wonderful, way better for him than Mom was. Iris was all he ever needed, and he hasn't paid much attention to anyone else since."

"Seems to be the way these things work."

"Sometimes. Maybe we make mistakes the first time and when the connection comes again it's more. More powerful. More important."

The question about Christina's ex came to mind, but in some way, he knew better than to ask in that moment. "So… what happened? With Iris?"

Christina's expression went slack, and her eyes dropped. "Cancer."

"I'm sorry."

"It hasn't been easy, but we have to figure things out. Keep moving, I guess."

Clint nodded and picked up the deck of cards. He dealt, then eyed the front door.

Christina reached for her cards. "You okay?"

"Yeah." Clint fanned his cards out in front of him.

"You sure about that?"

Clint frowned from one side of his mouth. "Think I'm tryin' to decide if I want to test the 'pretty much' comment."

Christina raised one eyebrow and settled back in her chair. "Only one way to find out?"

Clint tossed two cards down beside the resting deck, then sorted the four that remained in his hand. "Your…I guess I don't know what to call it. Kieran's dad. It didn't feel right asking at the time, but he said somethin' about him bein' out of the picture. That, and Duncan. Guess it set some gears turnin'."

"Oh." Christina set two cards on top of Clint's, then laid the rest of her hand face down on the table. "Maybe it's a typical story. I was young and didn't know what I wanted out of life. Or I didn't consider what I *would* want."

Clint got caught staring at Christina's ring finger.

She held her hand out to consider it before grabbing her whisky glass. "Never made it that far. But, by the time I figured out we weren't good for each other, that I should leave, Kieran was already with me."

Clint nodded. "I'm sorry." He straightened. "I mean, about the relationship. Not Kieran."

Christina held the back of her hand to cover her smile and shook as she held back a laugh, before she waved Clint's remark away. "I know what you meant." Soon her somber mood returned. "It wasn't easy, being on my own. I'm grateful that being here meant Kieran's had some good role models. Not that I didn't try and fill that position on my own. It's not always easy being a single mother. Some guys didn't understand that because of Kieran, they couldn't be the priority they wanted to be. Eventually, I guess, I just gave up on the whole situation."

Clint reached for his coffee cup. "Yeah, I get that. A little bit anyway." He drained the cup, then winced as the cold liquid hit his throat.

"I'm sorry that you do. Pretty sure it's not how we're meant to live."

Clint shrugged. "Maybe."

Christina sighed, easing forward in her chair and picking up her cards. She fanned them out, then dropped one face up in front of her. She focused her gaze on Clint. "Six."

# TWENTY-TWO

Brandon woke from a nightmare, though the details faded quickly under the commotion raging outside his room. Through the walls, through the floor, crashing, banging, and screaming echoed. Light from under the door radiated as if the sun had fallen to the ground just outside of it. That is, until an impact rocked the nearest fixture. It swung for a moment before it crashed and extinguished. Stomping feet thundered away down the hall. Whether to join the melee, or to escape it, was not at first clear.

Brandon pushed off from the wall next to his bed that he was bunched up against. As he moved to stand, his sweat-soaked legs caught on the sheets, and he nearly fell over. Steadied, he sat with his hands over his ears in an attempt to drown out the racket, while letting the coolness of the floor radiate up through the soles of his feet.

His door rocked against the latch when someone bounced off the other side. Someone else shouted as they careened down the hall. A torrent of obscenities, perhaps. If the noises were meant to be words at all, Brandon was not able to make them out.

Pressure rose behind his eyes. Blood pounding. Seething.

Brandon took a step toward the door, his fists clenched at his sides, his teeth grinding. He braced himself to launch into the hall, to chase down the inconsiderate pricks causing shit in the middle of the night, but before his first step made contact, his body hitched. He stumbled sideways, clutching at his stomach.

He propped himself up on the foot of his bed, body and head low, spit dripping and pooling at his feet. His torso shuddered, shoulders pinched together.

His chin dropped to his chest as he threw up a stream of black tar. He coughed and spit as the flow eased. The taste and smell berated his senses. He turned his head away and tilted his body, which only caused him to lose his balance.

Brandon lay on the floor, his body a loose curl. As the commotion outside continued, his muscles tensed. He brought one hand around and set his flat palm on the floor, squishing dark mess between his fingers. He raised bleeding eyes to the door and snarled.

# TWENTY-THREE

Christina smiled a little too wide. "Good game."

Clint tossed his counted hand on top of the deck, then leaned back with his arms crossed. "Yeah. Sure."

Christina pulled her pegs, then reached out for Clint's, further back on the board. "Dad usually gives me one hand, then takes the rest. He's been playing longer than I've been alive, but I'll get him honestly one day."

"Seems you can't be far off."

Christina's smile waned as she shrugged. "Maybe." She stashed the pegs and wrapped the cards back in their rubber band. Holding her smile, she drained her glass, then settled her eyes on Clint.

"Think it's time to head upstairs."

Clint rubbed at his face. "Yeah."

Christina stood and came around the table, her middle finger dragging along the edge. For support, or for show, Clint was not sure. At least, not at first.

Christina stood at the corner of the table, one leg crossed over the other, head tilted to her shoulder. The smile flared once again, but in an unsteady way. Her eyes were narrow but focused. "Any chance you'd like to join me?"

"Oh." Clint straightened in the seat. "Fuck."

Christina's expression soured. As she took in Clint's reaction, she stood rigid and crossed her arms high over her body. She turned without saying another word.

Clint shot up. "Christina, no, wait."

Christina stopped but did not turn to look at Clint.

"It ain't like that. It's just not where my head is at."

Christina scoffed. "It's not me, it's you."

"It ain't a line. I swear on my kids."

"It's fine." Christina set off for the stairs, nearly missing the first before she pulled herself up.

"I'm sorry…" Clint held the heel of both hands over his eyes until the creak of the stairs ceased. "Fuck." Lowering his hands, he exhaled and looked around the empty room. Feeling more out of place than alone, he moved toward the porch and stepped into his boots. He turned the lights off on his way out the door.

He stomped across the yard, head down against the wind and ice crystals digging into his skin. The shaking in his body as he traversed the stairs to the loft was more than just the chill in the air. He walked straight to his bed and sat, then hunched over on himself. As the barn creaked gently against the force of the wind, Clint pulled his hands from his eyes. Tears stained his cheeks and tracked down his neck. His body continued to shake as he tried to hold the pain in. He focused on a dark corner of the loft. A form tucked into the shadows. Not moving, but somehow, he felt it was watching him. He blinked his vision clear, but still the uncertainty remained.

With a tremor in his hands, he reached for the light beside his bed. The dim glow cast out, revealing cut timbers leaning up out of the way, a narrow roll of snow fence, and a couple lengths of rusting rebar.

Clint pushed himself against the short headboard, pulled his legs close, boots and all, then wrapped his arms over his knees. He shook and cried and stared at the corner.

In the early hours of the day his eyes closed, but he jerked awake at what could have been movement. He adjusted the lamp to better illuminate the collection propped up in the corner. He stayed that way until, once again, his eyes could finally stay open no more.

# TWENTY-FOUR

Brandon stood shoulder to shoulder with the other infected, jostling for space between the cold aluminum walls of a cattle liner, much like the livestock it was intended to contain. They uttered the odd grunt, but nobody spoke, the urge to fight each other muted by their collective transformation or used up after what it took to get them herded aboard. Either way, their attention and ire found a new point of focus.

Brandon could not see the men outside on the ground, both because of where he stood, and the errant snowflakes that crackled like fireworks as they blew past. It was easy enough to hear their grating voices, though, and even smell them above the abusive aroma of the pig shit he was standing in.

The heavy, sweating one, a security lead with the camp, spoke first. "Took you long enough to get here."

"Listen, just because it's been a couple months since your last outbreak, don't mean I'm just sittin' around waitin' for you to call." The skinny one, clouded with the scent of stale cigarettes and cheap beer, spit onto the gravel at his feet.

"'Sides, it's the middle of the goddamned night, and in case you ain't noticed, the roads are already turning to shit."

"Yeah, well, that ain't my problem." The heavy one ripped a page free from the clipboard in his hand. "Here's the rec. You'd better get a move on, the processing facility was expecting you an hour ago."

The skinny one snatched the piece of paper. The processing facility being an abandoned mine site. A place where nobody asked questions, because it was understood they would not like the answers. "What's it gonna be this time? 'Nother faulty heat exchanger?"

"Hell if I know. That's above my paygrade. Anyway, I think that's what they blamed the last one on."

The skinny one looked over his shoulder, sussing out movement between the open ports along the side of the trailer. "Seems this round caught more'n I've seen in a while."

The heavy one sighed. "Unfortunately." He hooked a thumb over his shoulder. "Two dead back there, which complicates things. Theory is it wasn't a local strain. Who knows if it'll actually be confirmed."

"Can't imagine they will." The skinny one eyed the flood lights over the yard, and the cameras hiding among the halos. "Not sure why you or anyone else hangs around to put up with this shit."

"Same reason you keep backing your truck up every time we call." The heavy one rubbed his pointer and middle finger back and forth across his thumb, then turned to go inside.

The skinny one averted his eyes and nodded. Without another word, he walked the length of the trailer, double-checked the latch on the door at the back, then went up the other side. Brandon and the others turned in place, acting as compass needles for his journey, right up until he stepped up into the cab and slammed the driver's-side door.

Brandon winced at the sound of the truck's engine as it rumbled to life, then braced his stance as the trailer lurched and jerked its way past the camp's security fence and lumbered off into the dark, snowy night.

TWENTY-FIVE

Jack looked up to the dark morning sky. Clouds and scattered snowflakes obscured any hint of time, so he shook his watch down his wrist to check it. He pushed out a breath through pinched lips, then focused back out the window.

Slow footsteps padded down the stairs soon after. A coffee cup turned over on the counter, then had a splash of coffee poured into it. The cupboard above opened. The lid of a bottle of drugstore brand aspirin clicked off, and two pills were shaken out before it was replaced.

"Good mornin'."

Christina popped the pills into her mouth, sipped at her coffee, then cleared her throat after she had swallowed them down. "If you say so."

Jack allowed a crooked smile as he checked over his shoulder. "Late night?"

Christina turned over a second mug and filled it near full. "Could have been." She walked over to her father and held the mug out.

Jack took it and drank. "Gonna be a bit of a late start."

"Sorry."

"Didn't mean it as condemnation."

"If you say so."

Jack turned to Christina with one eyebrow raised.

Christina side-eyed her father as she took another sip. She rested the mug on her flat palm. "Sorry."

"Seems to be the word of the day."

Christina opened her mouth to say it again but stopped in time.

Jack took another swig of his coffee before setting it on the kitchen table. "If you're okay to start breakfast, I'd like to head out and check the animals."

Christina nodded. "Yeah, of course."

"At your own pace. We should get some of that bread used up, though."

"Will do."

Jack nodded, then went to the porch to put on his heavy jacket and boots. Christina topped up her coffee, then leaned back against the counter to drink it.

# TWENTY-SIX

The skinny one hunched over the steering wheel, hands gripping it tight, bony elbows out wide. The only time he released the wheel was to change the speed on the windshield wipers. No matter how fast they moved, the view through the flat glass of the windshield refused to improve. Ice built up on the outside while the inside fogged around the edges.

In the trailer, Brandon and the others swayed along with the ruts on the patchy road and the driver's inconsistent path. That is, until the path disappeared.

Whether because of the impaired view, or snow covering the roadside signs, the truck and its occupants blew through a stop sign at a t-intersection.

The truck bucked against the trailer as it rocketed through the ditch and pitched sideways, nearly disconnecting as it slammed into a wooden power pole, snapping it loose from the ground in the process.

As it fell, wires snapped and snaked, showering sparks over the truck and the clumps of dead grass surrounding it not covered in the storm's fresh snowfall. The sparks smoldered before they began to burn.

## TWENTY-SEVEN

Jack shut the front door, stomped his boots, then unzipped and shook his jacket to get the snow off. When he removed his hat, light from the kitchen fixture reflected off the shiny red on his ears and nose. He didn't say a word as he walked into the house and to the phone on the wall between the entrance and the bathroom. He lifted the receiver to his ear, pressed down on the switch twice, then set the receiver back in its cradle.

Christina stopped chopping boiled potatoes and stood with the knife out to her side. "Everything okay?"

Jack stared at the floor as he ran a hand down his face. "Not sure. Heard somethin' big. Not an explosion exactly, but close." He motioned to the phone. "Line's dead."

Christina set the knife on the cutting board, wiped her hands on the tea towel next to it, then reached to her back pocket for her cell phone. A single bar flickered in and out of view.

Footsteps pounded up the porch steps and the front door swung open. May slid inside with Porter right behind her. He wiped the top of his head to rid it of moisture, then looked up to Christina and Jack staring at him, waiting.

"You heard the crash?"

Jack nodded. "If that's what it was."

Porter motioned in the direction of the trailers out back. "Power's out at the Dunns' place."

"It's out?"

"Not a single light on in the yard or house from what I could see. I smelled smoke, too."

"Like a fireplace?"

Porter shook his head.

Jack shuffled his feet and set his hands on his hips.

Porter looked from Jack to Christina and back. "What are you thinking?"

"Not much that's good." Jack chewed on his bottom lip. "Best if we bring everyone to the house. Figure things out from there."

The door opened again. Andie and Patch shuffled inside. Patch searched the expectant eyes watching him.

"Looks like we've got a good start, then." Jack moved to the kitchen window and crossed his arms. "Anyone heard from Odell or Duncan?"

Patch shook his head. "No, sorry."

Porter turned to May. "Stay. I'll be right back." He leaned forward. "Neghanighita."

May reached up for a kiss. "Hurry. Please."

Porter rushed out the door.

Jack watched as Porter hustled through the gap in the fence. "Anyone stop in at the barn?"

Andie and Patch shared a glance.

Jack looked over after his question was met with silence. "Sorry. I meant Clint." He turned his eyes to the light over the kitchen table. "I'm sure everythin' else is fine. For the moment."

Christina's shoulders slumped. She tucked her phone back in her pocket. "I'll go."

Jack bent his chin to his chest as his eyebrows pinched together. "What for? I can take care of it. I'm all ready to go, after all."

"It's fine. I can do it." Christina cleared her throat. "I need to do it."

Jack searched Christina's expression, unsure of what he was missing.

Christina did not acknowledge her father as she walked across the kitchen and toward the porch. Everyone stepped out of Christina's way as she rushed past, but she stopped before walking through the front door. "Do I need to check the gate?"

Jack shook his head. "All taken care of."

Christina nodded, slipped a long jacket on, then headed outside.

# TWENTY-EIGHT

The passenger-side door of the rig snapped open like a hatch to a secret bunker. One hand reached up, then another, and soon the skinny one pulled himself up and out of the cab, which was crooked and crumpled. He grunted and groaned his way down the exposed chassis, then took a few steps up past the ditch to flat ground. He sat between patches of burning grass and wiped blood from his eyes. The gash from his temple to his crown, opened to the bone, glittered with flecks of shattered glass. He looked from his bloodied and shaking hands over his shoulder to the cattle liner, lying on its side. The rear door was broken on its hinges and sat at an angle on the ground.

The driver dug in his jeans for a scratched up lighter, then patted his chest pocket for a pack of cigarettes that were not there. He slammed his fist into the cold ground. *"Fuck."* He turned his head as his bottom lip began to quiver. That was when the first of the infected hit him.

They tangled and rolled down the ditch as the skinny one screamed and fought to free himself. The other occupants of the trailer, those still mobile at least, flooded over to join the assault. Soon the driver was quiet, his mangled body camouflaged against the red stain growing around it.

Bruised, bleeding, and broken, the infected stood in the wind and the snow, scanning all around.

One in the group, with a broken arm hanging limp at his side, turned to face something through the trees.

A light. The only light that could be seen outside of the sparks and fire surrounding them. When he started walking, some of the others followed, but not all.

Brandon looked to the few of the infected that broke away from the horde, scattered into the fields, all heading in random directions. Seeking escape. He watched until they disappeared in the dark, then he followed the group heading toward the light.

# TWENTY-NINE

Christina eased up the stairs to the barn's loft. She stood a moment in the dark while she pulled out her phone and swiped to the flashlight app. She kept it low but swept it across the floor and the first of the empty beds, then the next. Soon she came to Clint, sitting up in bed, head leaned over on one shoulder, mouth hanging open in a soft snore. Her eyes moved ahead of the light, chasing a noise in the far corner. She caught a glimpse of eyes glowing like pinpoints and a slow, bared smile.

*"What the fuck?"*

She stumbled back, holding an arm out for balance while she swept the light over the corner and the entire space between.

A lamp clicked on.

Clint had one foot on the floor and an annoyed look on his pale face. "What are you doing?"

Christina glanced at Clint before focusing on the back corner. The stark light from her phone reached out into the darkness to show…a roll of snow fence and a couple timbers standing on end.

"Sorry. It's just…I thought I saw…" She switched the phone to her other hand. "Must have been one of the cats. Scared the shit out of me."

"Yeah. Cats." Clint rubbed at his eyes and shook his head to clear the cobwebs. "What time is it?"

Christina looked to her phone before turning the flashlight off. "Just after seven." She tucked it in her pocket. "Is it okay to turn the lights on?"

Clint stifled a yawn and nodded. With the flick of the wall-mounted switch, he squinted against the brighter light.

They each found something to look at. Christina the floor. Clint the far corner.

"Is there a reason for the wakeup call?"

"Uh, yeah. Power's out. Dad wants everyone inside."

Clint opened one eye to the lamp beside him, then closed them again. "Right. Off-grid."

Christina stepped forward, not looking directly at Clint, but in his direction. "Listen. About last night—"

"Really, it's—"

"—just wanted to say I'm sorry—"

Clint lowered his head. "I promise you ain't got nothin' to be sorry about."

"No. Just listen. Please."

Clint nodded but didn't look up.

"It's just…I don't know. It's lonely out here sometimes. Not that that's an excuse." Christina sighed. "I don't mean this the way it might sound, but I tend to have a thing for the ones that've seen some shit, you know? The broken ones, I guess."

Clint chewed on the inside of his cheek. "Yeah, well, guess I tick all those boxes."

"No, I didn't mean…" Christina shuffled her feet. "Christ. Anyway, I'm sorry, is the point of it all."

"I said it's fine. We're fine. I hope. I didn't mean to give the wrong impression is all."

Christina gave a sad smile. "Well, okay. Coffee's on. Let's go."

Clint looked down at the clothes he had been in for almost twenty-four hours.

"Don't worry about that, once the family meeting is over you can head for a shower."

"Doesn't sound as serious as your visit makes it out to be."

"That is to be determined."

Clint rubbed at his face again. "Just…can I have, like, thirty seconds?"

"Sure." Christina turned. "I'll wait for you downstairs."

———

Once Christina was down the steps, Clint stood. He took in a deep breath through his nose and pushed it out through his mouth. He glanced over his shoulder to the far corner of the loft but quickly looked away. He double-checked that Christina was out of sight, then turned to reach under his pillow. He tucked his pistol under his jacket, shut the bedside lamp off, then walked fast to the stairs.

Christina was outside the barn, holding the door. Once Clint had walked through, she shut and latched it, then fell in beside as he traversed the path to the house. They both kept their shoulders up to their ears and heads low as the wind swirled around them.

Footsteps and chatter caught Clint's attention, even as the

cold whistled through bare tree branches and over the roof peaks. He glanced toward the shop, then stopped.

Odell and Duncan shuffled through the weather on their way to the house, with Porter trailing behind.

The rifle tucked in the crook of Odell's arm gave Clint pause. As he eased around to continue on his way, though, something else caught his attention.

A figure, shedding steam from their exposed skin, charged forward between the western fence that marked the property line and the left side of the shop.

And they weren't alone.

# THIRTY

Clint's feet froze solid to the ground.

Christina's thundering footsteps as she sprinted to the house and up the porch steps barely registered. Neither did the first of the infected as they entered the halo of the yard lights.

The man reached out as he tripped on the transition between the uneven ground and the gravel path. The blood-soaked fingers of his good arm grazed Clint on his way past.

Clint did not move. He did not even flinch. His eyes stayed wide and stark, even as the world erupted around him.

Before the second of the infected reached Clint, Porter launched into them, shoulder first, laying them out on the ground.

Porter rolled and came up as the first was regaining his footing. A sharp uppercut bent the man's head back. The clack of his teeth echoed out. His body went limp and folded to the cold ground.

Porter looked to Clint but saw little in his catatonic eyes. Porter grabbed the shoulders of Clint's jacket and shook him. "You need to move. *Now.*"

Clint blinked. He looked at Porter, nodded, then reached under his jacket. He held the gun loose at his side.

Porter stepped back and shook his head.

Clint focused on the trees, the gap between the fence and the shop, the infected moving into the yard and those still huddled and waiting in the shadows. He raised his gun with an unsteady hand instead of focusing on the count.

Porter reached out, covering Clint's hand and slowly pushed the aim of the gun down. He stepped to stand in front of Clint and searched his pallid expression. "Listen, I know you think that's the response needed here. I see it. But trust me when I say you need to get out of the way and leave this to me."

Clint blinked and focused on Porter. Odell and Duncan crouched behind the right-hand corner of the shop, and the rest of the family huddled around the front porch or stared out from the front window.

Porter set a hand on Clint's shoulder and turned him toward the shed next to the old barn. "Go."

Clint stumbled away, collapsing among tall, dried grass.

Porter stepped into the path of the incoming mob, stood tall, and spread his hands wide.

The man, now in the lead, wearing grease-stained and bloodied coveralls, slowed and stopped three meters away. His eyes, crusted with rings of blood, bored into Porter's. He tilted his head back and to the side, searching for a scent on the erratic breeze. After a moment, his posture relaxed, and his fists unclenched, if only a little.

Porter lowered his arms and let out a long breath, the warmth swirling and dissipating over his head. He shifted his gaze to the porch, and Jack.

Jack stood, chewing on his bottom lip, searching the dark sky. He sighed and pointed to the old barn.

Porter checked over his shoulder, then looked back to Jack with his eyebrows pinched together and a scowl on his lips. He waved a hand to get Jack's attention, then spoke low. "We *don't* have room."

Jack whispered through gritted teeth. *"Figure it out."*

The group of infected turned as one. The man in coveralls snarled and took a step in Jack's direction.

Porter raised his arms again and got in between them to draw his attention. He locked eyes with the man, lowered one of his arms, and with the other, redirected to point at the old barn.

May squeezed past the family gathered on the porch and trotted down the steps. She squinted into the snow and wind, keeping one eye over her shoulder as she crossed the yard. At the old barn, she unlocked and pulled the big door aside. Red light flooded out, but nobody who would have found that unusual could see it. She cupped her hands to her mouth and called out, then ran back to the house. The man in coveralls snapped his focus on May and started forward.

Porter stepped in front of him again, waited until he confirmed his attention along with that of the group, then slowly turned and walked toward the open barn door. On his way, he knelt to weave his arms under the unconscious man, lifted him, then continued on.

Porter took the unconscious man to the very back of the barn and propped him up against the wall. He then waded through the infected as they filtered in. One or two bristled at the contact, but not enough to set them off. After the last of the infected was inside, Porter slid the door halfway closed.

With the newcomers contained, the family came out into

the yard. Andie continued on to the barn, and to Porter. Christina broke loose from the others and ran to Clint. She knelt next to him and adjusted the strap of the rifle over her shoulder. "Are you okay?"

Clint blinked but did not respond.

Christina reached out to grab his arm. "Come on. You should—"

At the end of the driveway, the sound of tearing metal announced the locked gate snapping open. Engines roared as an armored truck and two APP cruisers with stark headlights glaring careened into the yard.

# THIRTY-ONE

The APP armored truck skidded to a halt close enough to those standing in the yard that they took steps back in case it did not stop at all. A cruiser flanked either side of it without red-and-blue lights, without sirens. Doors flew open and the yard flooded with armed constables in protective armor. Shrouded in the glaring lights, one shouted, *"Weapons on the ground."*

Christina checked the safety on her rifle, then dropped it in front of her.

Jack pulled the rifle over his shoulder forward. He held it out, scanning the intricate inlay.

*"Now."*

Jack squinted into the harsh lights and crouched. He set his grandfather's rifle on the cold ground, considered the disgrace of it, then rose up to stand.

Clint pushed deeper into the shadows. He looked over to the old barn, and the sliver of red light coming out the open door. Through the swirling snow, he thought he saw a face, long, matted hair, and a beckoning hand. He tried to stand and run but only managed to crawl.

The passenger door of the cruiser closest to the house opened. "Evenin', Jack." Sergeant Spannhake stepped through the beams of the cruiser's headlights. He held one hand at his hip, the other adjusted the brim of his APP-issued baseball cap. His clean-shaven, square jaw was tight. "Long time no see. I only wish it weren't under such unfortunate circumstances."

Jack risked a glance around. His lips were drawn. "Not a great night to be out in the weather, I'll give you that."

Spannhake smiled. "The weather. Right." He hooked his thumb over his belt and motioned to the ground at Jack's feet with the other. "Is the weather why you're all out carrying long guns at this early hour?"

Jack looked in the direction of the pasture and pinched his lips to one side.

"Coyote."

"Coyote?"

"Yeah, four legs and a tail."

Spannhake laughed. "I'm aware of what a Coyote is, Jack."

Jack raised a hand, but slow. "Spotted one when I was out checking the herd earlier." He looked back to Spannhake. "Got to protect the herd."

"Okay, now we're getting somewhere." Spannhake came two steps closer. "You're certain it doesn't have anything to do with the wrecked cattle liner a couple hundred yards due north-west?"

Jack flushed. "You're sayin' you done busted up my gate over missin' livestock?"

Spannhake tilted his head, but his smile remained. "Livestock. Is that what you call them?"

Jack opened his mouth to respond but the words did not come.

Spannhake stepped closer. His smile waned as he traced the worn and red-tinged path in the thin snow cover. "You know, Jack, I've always had a feeling that something wasn't right about this place. About you, even though you all have done a fairly good job of staying under the radar." Spannhake stepped forward again, bringing him almost within reach of Jack. "Until now, that is." He pushed his tongue to the corner of his mouth and stared at the rifle on the ground as snow collected among the intricate details. "So, Jack, would you like to change your story?" Spannhake's smile returned, but it held little joy. "I'll give you one chance."

Jack's chin trembled. He glanced over his shoulder to the house, to the pasture, to the row of gun barrels trained on him. Everywhere but to the old barn. He cleared his throat. "Ain't no story to change."

Spannhake's teeth showed through his smile. His eyes focused on Jack, but his head stayed low. "We have a tradition around these parts, Jack, one I'm sure you're familiar with." He thumbed the snap on his holster. "When trouble comes around, you're supposed to shoot, shovel, and shut up."

Spannhake drew his service revolver and leveled it between Jack's eyes, then he pulled the trigger.

Christina wailed and dropped to her knees as her father crumpled in front of her.

At the fence dividing the front yard from the back, Odell took a single shot that went wide, extinguishing a spotlight on the armored truck.

One of the many bullets fired in retaliation pierced his

neck, just above his clavicle. He dropped the rifle and fell to his knees, clutching at the hole in his neck. He spit up a wad of deep red, then fell over on his side.

"*Odell.*" Duncan dropped to the ground. He grabbed Odell's leg and the rifle strap, then dragged both back around the nearest tractor for cover. Sporadic gunfire cratered the frozen ground around him and splintered the wooden fence.

Christina stumbled as Patch pulled her away from her father, up the porch steps, and into the house. May slammed the door and locked it behind them. Then the yard lights went out.

# THIRTY-TWO

Clint slipped through the old barn's door and pulled it closed as gunfire erupted outside. He did not have a chance to turn before the hair on the back of his neck raised.

The air was dense with an all-too-familiar smell, like rotting meat with a coppery tinge.

Clint spun and pressed his back to the door.

The space inside was smaller than it looked from the outside. The walls were clad in plywood with plastic sheeting showing through the gaps. Each side of the barn had three stalls stretching to the back. Instead of wooden barriers, they each had tall chain-link doors enclosing them. Ventilation fans were mounted high to one side, and dim, red lights lined the ceiling.

Clint's breath fogged as he ejected short, anxious bursts, but it was nothing like the group of the infected huddled together at the opposite end of the barn.

Four stood in the aisle, seven or eight others leaned out to watch him from the open stalls on either side.

Clint patted his pocket without looking down, confirmed

which the gun was in, then pulled it out and pointed it at the ground in front of him.

"Clint."

The voice came so gently it took Clint a moment to register it. He glanced to his left.

Porter stood in the narrow cove at the base of the ladder that led to the loft above. He held one flat palm out. "It's okay. Put it down."

Clint looked to the gun in his hand as if he'd never seen it before. He lowered it but gripped it tightly as his eyes twitched to the infected.

"That's better."

The chain-link door to his right creaked open, and Andie stuck her head out. "What's going on?"

"Not sure yet. Clint's a little freaked out." Porter leaned down to better be in Clint's field of vision. "Clint? What's happening out there?"

Clint shook his head, swallowed. "Cops."

Porter's jaw tightened.

Clint's eyes never left the back of the barn. "What the *fuck* is this?"

Andie pushed the door all the way open and stepped out of the opening. She beckoned Clint closer. "Let me show you."

Clint hesitated, but focused on Andie's soft eyes, and stepped forward. He leaned around the edge of the opening and peered inside. The stall held a narrow bed, a fold-out table and chair, a portable toilet like you would take camping, and a hand sink tucked in the corner. It was set up like a camper, or like a jail cell. A man sat on the bed, hands clutched in his lap, eyes flittering between Clint and Andie. He looked pale, even in the red light. Gaunt. His eyes were dark, bloodshot.

"Clint, this is my son, Kenneth."

Clint swallowed as the last of the moisture in his throat disappeared. "But…he's…"

"Yes. He is." Andie stepped back and swung the door closed, then latched it. She wove her fingers through the chain-link. "Goodnight, my son. Momma loves you."

Kenneth's mouth opened, but no sound came.

Andie turned to Clint, moisture building in her eyes. "This is why we're all here. Acceptance. Safety. The world thinks one thing when people get sick like this, but it's not just one thing. Kenneth isn't well enough to be out on his own, but we were so fortunate to have the opportunity to join Jack and his family. Nothing is perfect in this world, but they have a space of their own." She motioned overhead. "The lights help keep them calm."

Clint stepped back into the door. "Okay."

"Kenneth is the last. Or could be. Iris only left us a few months back now. Odell and Duncan's parents passed a few months before that."

"Wait." Clint's eyes shifted back and forth as he processed. "Iris? You mean…"

"Jack's second wife. Yes. She's the reason for all of this. He wanted a place to keep her close."

"But…" Clint focused on Porter's bloodshot eye. "Oh, fuck."

"Now don't be like that."

Porter adjusted the ear buds in his ears, then crossed his arms.

"Porter's fine. Fine enough not to be stuck in here at any rate."

One of the infected snarled and lunged after an orange cat that scrambled out from one of the stalls. Clint shifted like he was ready to run, but his flight instinct could not choose between bad and worse.

Andie scuttled to the back waving her hands. *"No."* She slapped the infected man on his shoulder and wagged a finger in front of his face. "You leave them alone."

The man braced to attack but held his ground.

Andie waved him back. "Go. Get back with the others."

The man tilted his head, dropped his shoulders, then stepped backward.

Andie offered one last stern look. "That's better. Now, what on earth is going on out there?"

Porter's expression hardened. He pushed past Clint and opened the door only enough to confirm the scene in the yard. He slid the door closed but kept his grip on the handle. "Dammit."

"What is it?"

"APP. More of them than is good for us." He took one last look before closing the door as quietly as he could. He lowered his eyes. "Jack…he's…"

Andie held shaking fingers to her mouth. "He's what?"

Porter closed his eyes and shook his head.

"Oh no…" Tears fully formed in Andie's eyes. She wiped them as she looked up to Porter. "What do we do?"

Clint's whole body began to shake as he absorbed the full extent of his situation.

Porter looked to the infected at the back of the barn. "Might only be one thing we can do."

# THIRTY-THREE

May slammed the front door and drew the deadbolt, then set the lock plate at the bottom. Patch kept one hand in front of him, pushing Christina as she shook and sobbed through the house. With the other hand he flipped light switches, turning off the exterior lights on the outside of the house and in the yard, and interior lights as they went. May followed toward the back of the house but diverted through the door to the basement while Patch moved Christina into the living room.

Kieran stood at the bottom of the stairs leading to the upper level, his eyes wide and lips tight. He glanced out the kitchen window on his way past as he followed Patch and his mother. He stopped with his arms out, gripping each side of the door frame that opened to the living room. "What's going on?"

Christina sat in Jack's recliner with her rifle propped against the wall beside. She held herself while she rocked back and forth. Tears streamed from her red eyes and snot dripped down her parted lips.

Patch drew all the curtains, then turned to the boy. "I'm afraid our special situation here has been found out."

Kieran snuck a glance over his shoulder. "Where's Grandpa?"

Patch lowered his eyebrows and pushed his bottom lip up into his top. "I'm sorry, son. He…"

Kieran dropped his arms. "No." He turned to the front of the house, but Patch rushed forward to stop him before he got far.

"Wait. Please."

Kieran turned with tears in his eyes.

"Your granddad knew something like this might happen. He had a plan in place, and right now we need to keep you safe."

"But we need to fight back."

"We need to do something else first."

Kieran wiped at his face with one hand, then the other. "What does that mean?"

Patch placed a hand on the boy's shoulder as May came into the room, a lever-action rifle and a tall backpack strung over her shoulder, a rifle case and a bag that jangled with boxes of shells in her hands. "It will be easier if we show you, but we have to get out of here first."

# THIRTY-FOUR

When the yard lights went out, Sergeant Spannhake was left standing in the halo cast by the half-circle of police vehicles idling in the cold. He scanned all directions before turning to the group of constables waiting on orders.

"Foss and Nowicki, you're with me. Barton and Turcotte, check to make sure you did your job with the two behind the fence. You three,"—he bobbed a flat hand at his side—"hold tight a minute."

Spannhake walked over Jack's body without looking down and moved deeper into the yard. Constable Foss and Nowicki flanked him but stayed one step behind. Spannhake stood with his hands at his waist while he scanned the dark windows of the house. "It's important to note that what's happening here was entirely in your control. All of it. All you had to do was listen to what you were told. I want you to remember that." He turned in place. A smile crept across his face. He tilted his chin over his shoulder and shouted into the wind. "But that's not what the headlines will read tomorrow.

It'll be more like, family dies in tragic fire due to faulty solar panel wiring. Something like that, anyway."

Spannhake walked toward the back of the yard. He raised his service revolver and fired twice at the galvanized overhead fuel tank. Purple gas spewed onto the ground and trickled away in all directions.

He stepped closer, then reached inside his coat and under his ballistic vest for the half-empty packet of cigarettes in the chest pocket of his shirt. He pulled a lighter from his pants pocket. With a cigarette perched on his lips, he rolled his thumb over the top of the lighter and cupped a hand around the low flame to protect it.

Spannhake drew hard twice to make sure the cigarette was lit, then held it out in front of him. He watched the bright glow at the end for a moment before flicking it to the ground. It landed in an expanding pool of gasoline and immediately fizzled out. Spannhake tilted his head to one side. "Well shit."

The report from a rifle echoed from the back half of the yard, followed by shouted commands, and the pop and snap of rounds fired in response. Foss and Nowicki spun and raised their weapons. Spannhake glanced in the general direction, but no real concern showed on his face.

Across the yard, Turcotte stumbled backward into view. He fired into the dark. Another rifle blast called out, and Turcotte's head jerked back. He fell sideways, a wet hole where his left eye used to be. From around the corner, three shots from a handgun punctuated the interaction, then all fell quiet.

Spannhake waited until shuffling along the ground manifested in Constable Barton with a hand tight against the wound on his leg. He looked over to Spannhake but kept moving to the nearest cruiser.

Spannhake rolled his eyes. "Well, now that's taken care of…where was I?" He turned back to the overhead fuel tank, still leaking gas everywhere. "Right."

He lit a second cigarette, held it to his side, then looked to the lighter in his hand. He shrugged. "Let's see how this goes." He took a drag, kneeled, and struck the lighter again.

The flame caught immediately and expanded like a shockwave. Spannhake jerked back in response, almost falling on his ass. The flame chased around the woodshed to the left of the fuel tank and over to the edge of the old barn. It raced under the fence that divided the front yard from the back and expanded toward the new barn as well.

Spannhake turned away and took a single, long drag from the cigarette before flicking it into the night. "That's better." His smile grew wider as he walked toward the cruisers. It did not last, though.

Porter was past the threshold of the old barn before the door had fully opened. As he thundered forward, the infected spilled out behind him.

He swung a hard fist at the closest constable. The punch shifted Nowicki's jaw, and everything attached to it, forty-five degrees before the sound of it faded. The light in his eyes extinguished before his body hit the ground.

Gunfire erupted as the infected fanned out. Foss managed to fire twice before being tackled.

Spannhake edged closer to the cruisers and carefully placed bullets through the skulls of the infected clawing and beating Foss.

Porter broke the arm of one of the constables before he was shot in the side. He rolled around back of the armored truck and tucked himself underneath while the constable fired an insufficient number of bullets at inbound infected with his non-dominant hand.

When the gunfire ceased, Spannhake and Constable McCarthy stood with their backs to each other. Foss kneeled on the ground, bleeding from scratches on his face and hands. Across the yard, Barton leaned against the hood of the armored vehicle fumbling to release a fresh clip from his vest.

Twelve dead infected bled out on the ground around them.

Spannhake spread his feet wide apart and let his arms hang by his sides, gulping air to satiate his need for oxygen. He looked to the barn, the open doorway glowing red and rimmed with fire. Inside, a shadowy figure stepped forward.

Spannhake raised his gun and bared his teeth. He squeezed the trigger.

The hammer clicked on an empty chamber.

# THIRTY-FIVE

Brandon stopped before the threshold of the barn and stared out into the dark.

Sergeant Spannhake, sweating in his uniform despite the cold, scowled and raised a gun in Brandon's direction. The sound of the hammer dropping echoed through Brandon's skull. The fire. The smell of sweat and burning fuel and wood. Brandon looked around at the bodies littering the ground. The pressure in his head, the rage, overwhelmed him. He attacked.

He hit Spannhake as he was turning to run. Brandon pinned him, back to the ground, knees grinding into the sergeant's arms.

Brandon wrapped his hands over Spannhake's head to hold it still. Gunfire erupted around them, but Brandon paid no attention.

Instead, he pressed his thumbs into the sergeant's eyes. Brandon pushed into the warmth, until he hit the second knuckle. Spannhake's scream kept changing pitch, like he was attempting to reach a tone where he could break glass.

Brandon, barely able to focus against the noise, finally had enough. He pulled his thumbs from Spannhake's eyes, then plunged his pointed fingertips into the sergeant's neck. He twisted and pushed until he had a grip on the sergeant's larynx, then he tore it free.

# THIRTY-SIX

Clint followed the last of the infected as they charged out of the barn. As Constable McCarthy sighted his weapon, Clint raised his gun in one unsteady hand and pulled the trigger four times in quick succession.

All but one hit the constable's vest, throwing McCarthy's balance off and causing him to fire wide in response.

In the time it took Clint to blink, a piece of himself he thought had broken forever slipped back into place. The bodies scattered all around. The relentless screaming. His free hand raised up to steady his aim. He squeezed the trigger once. McCarthy's body went limp as his own finger was about to squeeze.

Next, he sighted on Constable Foss as he kicked and crawled his way toward the end of the house.

Foss stopped, fighting for breath, then propped himself up to sit on his feet. He ran his hands over the broken and swollen skin on his face. He looked from the blood on his hands to each of the bodies around him. Those showing signs of infection, at least. Foss reached for the empty holster on his belt, then locked eyes with Clint.

Blood dripped from his trembling chin. "Please…"

Clint pulled the trigger one last time.

As Barton slammed a fresh clip home and steadied himself to intervene, his legs went out from under him, and he was pulled halfway beneath the front of the armored vehicle. Automatic gunfire beat an uneven staccato. Barton spit up a mouthful of blood before his head listed sideways. Though his eyes remained open, he was gone.

Clint ignored or did not hear the grunting and groaning that came from behind the headlights of the armored vehicle. Instead, his attention remained on the man standing over the now silent Sergeant Spannhake

Brandon hunched with his arms wide at his sides, and his exposed skin flaring steam into the air. His head turned to look over his shoulder. Fresh blood flecked his face, adding layers to the old.

Clint sighted his gun between eyes flickering with the fire crawling up the front of the barn.

They watched each other, for how long Clint wasn't sure, but he was the first to offer an end to the stalemate. He lowered his arm. The gun swung once at his side before it dropped to his feet.

Brandon broke his gaze away to scan the yard through the assault of glaring headlights, then he focused on the fence bordering the yard, and the pasture beyond. He turned to Clint one last time, dropped the ragged and dripping mass in his right hand, then walked off into the darkness and solitude.

"Clint?"

Clint tensed and spun around.

Andie stood next to Kenneth, their arms looped together.

She offered an urgent look. "Excuse us. It's getting a little warm."

Clint nodded and stood aside.

Andie and Kenneth passed by taking short, unsteady steps toward the house, though he could not tell who might have been supporting who. As they approached the porch steps, deep coughing rumbled across the yard.

Porter propped himself up against the armored vehicle, one hand flat against the wound on his side, the other wrapped around the handle of the automatic rifle resting on the hood but aimed in Clint's direction. "Is that all of them?"

Clint scanned the mess around him. "I...I don't..."

On the ground nearby, Constable Nowicki cradled his arms over his head as he slowly curled in on himself.

Clint looked from Nowicki to Porter. He tried to swallow, but the moisture in his throat seemed to want to only escape through the corners of his eyes.

Porter closed his eyes and sighed. He released the rifle, letting it slide down the hood and crash to the ground. "Leave him. Enough has been lost tonight."

Clint worked to clear his throat, though his voice was quiet. "Are...are you okay?"

Porter winced as he adjusted his lean against the hood of the armored vehicle. "Should be. Maybe."

Clint nodded, then looked away.

"Listen." Porter groaned as he pushed himself upright. "We need to get moving before backup arrives."

# THIRTY-SEVEN

Clint rushed up the stairs to the loft. Haze hovered around the exposed lights, but the fire had yet to break through. He shoved his possessions into his bag, lifted it over his shoulder, then turned to go. That was when the lights flickered and went out.

"Goddammit." Clint took careful steps, reaching out to keep himself from kicking bedframes on his way past. Near the middle of the loft, he stopped and listened. The barn creaked and groaned. The odd snap echoed around him. He looked to the far corner. It was just shadows and piled-up junk. He knew that. But whether because of the afterglow, or something else, he saw more.

"K...Krystal?"

Clint was not sure if he heard what he thought he did. Whether it was a voice or shifting of the structure around him.

"*Clint.*"

Tears welled in his eyes, though he did not wipe them away as they overflowed. "Krys. I...I don't know what's happening. To me. I...don't know what to do."

The floor creaked. *"What you avoid."* The walls groaned. *"Will find you."*

Clint's chin protruded as it trembled. He blinked hard in an unsuccessful attempt to clear the tears.

*"If you want to escape."* The loft door rattled in the wind. *"Stop running."*

Clint's body shook as he held the heels of his hands to his eyes.

"Clint?"

Clint dropped his hands, and the lights flickered back to life. May stood near the top of the loft stairs.

Clint wiped at his eyes then wiped his hands on his pants. "What?"

May scanned the empty loft. "We need to go. Now."

# THIRTY-EIGHT

When Clint reached the bottom of the narrow stairs, both the front and back doors of the barn were wide open and the stalls empty. Through the back, he caught a brief glimpse of the horses in the pasture with the odd chicken milling about as well. His pace toward the front yard slowed as he neared the break in the fence. For the first time he saw the shadowed forms of Duncan, face down on the ground, and Odell, slumped against the fence with his jaw slack.

Patch stood on the porch with a couple hastily packed suitcases and a pile of gun cases to his left, and two red gas cans to his right. Jack's truck idled outside the garage. Kenneth sat in the bed, not moving, just watching. What Clint presumed was Jack's body lay covered in a blanket, just inside the gate. Christina and Kieran stood holding each other at the back of the truck, the strap of Christina's great-grandfather's gun strung over her back. Christina brushed one hand down Kieran's hair and cheek.

Not knowing what else to do, Clint joined them. "What now?"

Christina wiped at her eyes. "Dad always knew something like this could happen. I just didn't think…" She wiped at her cheeks and steadied her chin. "There's a converted Sprinter van in the shop. Porter is loading up fuel and a few supplies. The lake should be frozen for the season, so we're going to cross it. There's an old ATV trail on the Saskatchewan side. As long as we keep our distance from the boundaries of the bomb range, we shouldn't find any unwanted attention. Either way, with only two roads in or out of this place, it's our best chance."

They stood without speaking, without looking at the bodies scattered all around, flickering light from the growing flames fighting to give warmth to cooling skin.

Clint sniffed, then turned to the distant darkness. "Well. I guess this is goodbye."

Christina focused on her hands as her fingers interlaced. "Not if we all go together."

It was Clint's turn to look at his hands. He chewed on his response, but not for long. "Maybe."

"Maybe?"

"I think I need to go home. See my kids." He looked over his shoulder to the new barn's loft. "Deal with some things."

Christina bit her bottom lip and nodded.

"Doesn't mean I won't be back. That I can't find you." He reached out to Christina. "I mean, if you still want me to."

Christina hooked her fingertips into Clint's. A smile flared but did not last.

Clint squeezed her hand in return, then turned it palm up. He took the burner phone from his jacket pocket and folded it into her fingers. "I'll call when I can."

Christina nodded. "I'll be waiting."

"Good." Clint adjusted the strap of his bag and tucked his

hands in his pockets. That was when the back corner of the old barn collapsed, sending sparks swirling into the gray, pre-dawn sky. "I guess that's our cue."

Behind them, May lifted the last of the suitcases and guns into the back of Jack's truck before climbing in herself.

Patch lifted a gas can in each hand and pushed the front door open with his foot. As dancing orange flames rose in the windows, Patch came back outside, closed the door, then went to join the others in the truck.

Christina kissed Kieran on his forehead and held his face in her hands. "Go jump in."

Kieran wiped at his face, briefly glanced to Clint, then walked off.

Christina sucked breath in through her nose to clear it and tucked her hands into the back pockets of her jeans. "Follow us to the back. There's an old trail that will take us to the next range road over. As long as the APP don't get their shit together too fast, we'll be far enough out before roadblocks start going up. Once you find the road south you can go wherever you need. They aren't looking for you, so you should be okay."

Clint nodded but diverted his attention to the fence. "What about Duncan and Odell? They're…"

"Don't worry. They won't be left behind."

Clint lowered his eyes. "I'll help get them loaded up."

"Thank you." Christina pursed her lips and turned to go.

"Christina. Wait."

She looked back.

"I'm sorry. About your dad. About all of this."

She nodded and blinked away fresh tears.

Christina stepped up behind the wheel of her father's truck, crammed in with Patch, Andie, and Kieran on the bench seat. Her great-grandfather's rifle spanned the dash, resting up against the windshield. She backed out to the main drive, then drove to the other side of the fence separating the front yard from the back. May jumped down to help Clint bring Duncan and Odell into the truck bed and under the blanket with Jack.

May closed the tailgate and brushed her hands down the front of Porter's jacket. "Be safe."

"You too. Tell Porter…just tell him thank you."

May nodded, then she hopped up into the bed and sat near the back window.

The big door on the shop opened as the truck passed, and Porter idled the Sprinter out behind them. Its matte-black paint matched the wheels. Solar panels covered the tall roof. Heavy bush bumpers and skid plates hung off both ends. Clint just caught a hint of the Saskatchewan license plate on the back as it drove off into the shadows and falling snow.

Clint turned himself to the east, and the first signs of the sun breaking above the horizon. A new day, but maybe, more than that.

Somewhere in the distance, a chorus of sirens pierced the calm. With nothing else to do, Clint turned to the break in the fence, and he ran.

**Thank you for reading!**

Reviews are extremely important to indie authors. They help us hone our craft and find new readers. If you enjoyed this book, please consider sharing your thoughts on Amazon, Goodreads, or BookBub.

———

———

**Also by Shane Kroetsch**

*This and That but Mostly the Other*
*Into the Storm (Book One of the Storm Series)*
*Surviving the Storm (Book Two of the Storm Series)*
*Chasing the Storm (Book Three of the Storm Series)*

# AFTERWORD

This book wasn't always meant to be a book. It started as a short story to be given away after Chasing the Storm was published in 2021. Then I thought it should be the updated ending to Chasing because I second-guessed the original cliffhanger. It wasn't until November of 2022 that I put the opening scene and a few other scribbled notes together with the intention of it becoming the fourth book in The Storm series. November 2022 was a long time ago, relatively speaking, but I've got some pretty good reasons why things have taken as long as they did.

I spent every minute of 2022 navigating change. My focus was building a new life. Not only new, but authentic. Eighteen months in, as things had started to level out, everything changed again, but in ways and magnitudes I could not have previously imagined.

In August of 2023, I lost my partner in life and creativity, my soulmate, Kaleigh Kanary. Lost feels like an insignificant word to explain the situation, but it accurately enough describes her passing, and for me, what came after.

I believe our identity is reflected in the people we love the most, and without my person beside me, I could no longer see who I was. I struggled with direction in my life and in my writing, both of which she was an integral part of. I struggled with what had meaning and what didn't. Eventually, I came to understand that what we all need to do, whether actively making friends with grief or not, is to keep moving forward. In our own way, at our own pace, and in our own direction. I had to accept that, sometimes, endings are new beginning in disguise. Not in spite of what came before, but as an act of love for the people and things that helped make us who we are. Kaleigh made me a better writer, and a better human being. Because of that, she will always be with me. She will always be part of this journey. Today and tomorrow. With this book, and the next one, and the one after that.

So that's why, after three years of moving forward but not moving on, of being on the path to rediscovering who I am, Escaping the Storm will be released. Yes, it's taken much longer than I initially hoped. But something else I've learned is that things in this life tend to happen in the time and ways they are meant to.

To Shayla, Michelle, and Taija, thank you for helping me make this story the best it can be. To you, dear reader, thank you for supporting my journey. It means more than you know.

# ABOUT THE AUTHOR

Shane Kroetsch is the author of dark stories that shine a light on the condition of being human. Except, sometimes there are monsters too… Over the past seven years he has released a collection of short fiction, a zombie outbreak series, and been featured in a growing number of anthologies. Shane lives, works, and creates in Alberta, Canada on the traditional and unceded lands currently labelled as Treaty 7 Territory and Métis Nation of Alberta Region 4.